RUNAWAY RABBIT

By the same Author:

    THE HEPZIBAH HEN BOOK.

    HEPZIBAH AGAIN.

    HENRY HEATHERKIN.

    THE ADVENTURES OF MR. WOGGINS.

    BEETLES AND THINGS.

    YOUNG YAP.

Uniform with this volume:

    TADDY TADPOLE.

" Too big ! " she said in a decided voice.

OLWEN BOWEN

RUNAWAY RABBIT

ILLUSTRATED BY L. R. BRIGHTWELL

THOMAS NELSON AND SONS, LTD.
LONDON EDINBURGH PARIS
TORONTO NEW YORK

CONTENTS

FULL-PAGE ILLUSTRATIONS

RUNAWAY RABBIT

CHAPTER I

ESCAPE

" It's no good grumbling," said Angelina. " It won't make any difference."

Sultan, the large Angora rabbit, said nothing at all. He wasn't grumbling. He hadn't grumbled. By means of great self-control he had managed to keep up a dignified silence, and now this silly rabbit was telling him not to grumble. Yes, silly rabbit Angelina, even if she was his sister.

" No, it's no good grumbling ! We shall just have to make the best . . ."

Bang !

Angelina's cheerful voice stopped suddenly in a high squeak of fear as a noise, which seemed as loud and sudden as a pistol shot, echoed round and round again inside the Shed. Startled rabbit faces pressed against the wire netting of the many hutches which lined the wall. Round, pink eyes gazed anxiously out, and rabbit whiskers twitched with curiosity to know whence the sudden noise had come.

But it was not a pistol shot. It was only Sultan—Sultan annoyed out of his dignified silence—Sultan stamping with rage upon the wooden floor of his hutch.

" How you startled me ! " gasped Angelina. " Oh dear, oh dear ! I feel quite upset ! " and, lowering her voice to a whimpering squeak, she hurried to the other side of her hutch, where she was soon busy discussing the coming Show in undertones with the rabbit next door.

With a grunt of relief Sultan turned away. Things were bad enough as it was without his having to listen to that foolish chatter. Another Show indeed ! Everybody knew that *he* was the finest rabbit in the neighbourhood, probably in the whole country. He'd proved it many times over. The wall above his hutch was plastered with certificates which said so in large black lettering. And yet they had to keep on doing it—more Shows, more brushing, more combing, more uncomfortable small boxes, more . . .

Sultan's thoughts were brought to an end by the sudden opening of the outside door of the Shed. Sultan looked up. He wasn't interested. He didn't care who it was—but he looked up.

In through the door, carrying a pail full of food and a bundle of fresh lettuce leaves, came Jane and Henry.

Sultan had no personal feelings about Jane and Henry. They were useful. They brought his food, cleaned his hutch out, sometimes even took him out in the run. But on the other hand they did a number of tiresome things with brushes and combs, and, worst of all, they were

responsible for this stupid Show business. No, Sultan did not think much of Jane and Henry.

"Too wet to take them out to-day," said Henry.

"Yes," agreed Jane. "And let's leave all the grooming till to-morrow, then we'll be able to pack them off early the next day for the Show."

As soon as the feeding business was over Jane and Henry left them for the night.

" Haven't even shut the door properly ! " grunted Sultan. No, he did *not* like Jane and Henry.

Slowly Sultan ate his supper. Thoughtfully he nibbled at the last remaining lettuce leaf. Through the unfastened door, now swinging open several inches on its hinges, he could see the soft green grass and, beyond, the unexplored hedge. All looked fresh, green, and cool after the recent rain. In comparison everything within the Shed seemed dull and uninteresting.

Suddenly Sultan stopped eating. He had had an idea ! And the more he thought of the idea the more he liked it. Once, long ago, he had found a way of raising the corner of the wire netting in front of his hutch so that he could push through it and jump down on to the floor of the Shed. He had done this several times and then Henry had found him, put him back into his hutch, and pushed the wire netting into place again with his fingers, saying that he must bring a hammer and nail it down. But Sultan had never climbed out again—the floor of the Shed had not been really interesting, and he disliked being picked up by Henry—and as far as he knew Henry had forgotten all about the hammer and nails. But now—now the door of the shed was open—*now* was altogether different.

Eagerly Sultan pushed his nose down to the corner of the hutch. No ! It had not been nailed. Once more the wire netting yielded, and a few seconds later Sultan jumped down to the floor.

For a moment he stood and listened. All was quiet inside the Shed. The other rabbits, having finished their suppers, were now fast asleep. Not one of them saw Sultan as he loped quietly across to the door, pushed his way through and, for the first time in his life, stepped out on to the grass and down the garden path, a FREE rabbit—an independent rabbit—and not just something shut up in a box and sent to a Show. No, the others might have to go—Angelina might go—silly rabbit Angelina—but not Sultan, the prize Angora.

CHAPTER II

MORE RABBITS

A LIGHT evening breeze swept softly across the country-side. Tall shoots of young corn dipped and rose again, rustling gently as the wind passed them by, while from the middle of the field came a louder rustle, a crackling sound as of something pushing, forcing its way through the forest of green stems. A moment later two pink ears, followed by a white head, thrust themselves above the level of the wheat.

"This is all very amusing," muttered Sultan, the prize Angora, " but I wish I knew where I was, and how to get somewhere else ! "

The head and ears disappeared. Sultan had seen a gate, and a little more pushing and rustling through the corn brought him to the edge of the field. A gate must lead somewhere ! Sultan squeezed his way underneath it, crossed another field, and found himself on the top of a steeply sloping bank.

"I've never seen anything like it before ! " said Sultan to himself. It was soft and grass-covered—a bank that no rabbit could resist running down—and so, pink ears alert to catch any strange sound, Sultan ran down to the bottom.

That was fun—the sort of thing to do again and again —and Sultan climbed slowly back to the top. On the way he passed a large, round, dark hole, almost hidden by the grass. At the bottom of the slope was a stony way with shining metal lines glittering in the evening sunlight. Everything was new—everything was strange. It was good to be a rabbit on an evening like this.

Sultan had almost reached the bottom of the bank for the second time when suddenly, from round the corner, came a noise which almost deafened him. The next moment, rushing, roaring, puffing towards him, came the largest and most terrifying monster Sultan had ever seen. Quick! It was almost on him! Up the bank scuttled Sultan, faster than he had ever run before. Up and up, then, to his horror, the frightened white rabbit caught his foot in a straying root, stumbled, fell, and then, more alarmed than he had ever been in his life, he felt himself beginning to roll rapidly down the hill, straight towards the roaring, rushing terror.

Still it came on, louder and nearer, clouds of smoke blowing away behind it. Over and over rolled Sultan. In a moment it would be upon him! Somehow Sultan managed to clamber to his feet. For a moment he stood dazed, not knowing which way to run. The noise was overpowering—everywhere was smoke.

" Come in here ! Come this way ! "

Somebody was speaking! Somebody was calling him. Sultan turned and rushed wildly in the direction of the unknown voice.

"This way! Down this hole."

Hardly knowing what he did Sultan plunged into the dark, round hole which he had noticed when he first came to the bank. Almost immediately the roaring of the monster behind him seemed to stop, and he found himself in a narrow, dark passage. In front of him, as well as he could see in the dim light, something seemed to be moving, and when he had followed it for several yards down the passage the voice spoke again.

"It wouldn't have hurt you really, you know," it said cheerfully. "It was only a train, and they happen quite often in the day. All the same I like to get out of the way of them myself. With that noise going on almost anything might happen. And I certainly shouldn't care to roll down the bank towards it the way you were doing. It isn't safe, you know."

Still gasping for breath Sultan tried to explain that he wasn't doing it for fun, that it had all been a very horrid accident, and he hoped he'd never see the hill again.

"I've never seen you there before," said the voice curiously, "and I thought I knew all the rabbits on the bank. My name's Bobbin, and this is where I live. Come in."

Sultan was beginning to enjoy himself. This was
(3,944)

what he called an adventure. This was being free, and
going about, and seeing things. He had heard that some
rabbits lived in burrows in the ground, and now here he
was, being invited into one of these homes by the funny
little brown rabbit which was standing in front of him.
It was a nice little brown rabbit, not handsome like him-

self, of course, but a friendly little brown rabbit, and
before he had been in the house two minutes Sultan
found himself telling Bobbin all about the Shed, and the
Show, and how he had only just managed to escape and
run away.

"Best thing you could have done," said Bobbin,
nodding his head: "and now I expect you'd like to see
the others. Lots of us live in this Warren, but I'm the

only one in now. The others are all in the wood.
We shall find them if we go out the back way. Come
along."

Sultan came along. He followed Bobbin down yards
and yards of dark twisting passage, sometimes so narrow
that he could hardly push his way through, sometimes so
low that, even with his long ears pressed tightly down
along his back, he feared he might not be able to squeeze
through. Bobbin, who was altogether smaller, had no
difficulty in getting along, and when at last the white
rabbit reached the mouth of the tunnel he found him
waiting at the foot of a tall tree on the edge of a
wood.

" Come along ! " he cried, and scampered off again,
not stopping until they came to a small clearing in the
middle of the wood. Here Sultan found, to his surprise,
that all around them were rabbits, dozens of rabbits,
brown rabbits with little white tails, just like Bobbin—
common rabbits Sultan thought, ordinary rabbits, not
in the least like the giant balls of fur he was used to
meeting at the Shows. A moment ago they had all been
moving about—jumping, running, chasing each other
round the trunks of trees—but now they stood, each one
still as a statue, round-eyed, anxious, staring and staring
fixedly at Sultan.

"It's all right ! " called out Bobbin. " It's only
Sultan ! He's quite friendly, and I've brought him to
see you."

Still the crowd of rabbits continued to stare. Never before had they seen anything at all like Sultan. Black rabbits they knew, brown rabbits there were plenty, but *white* . . .

At last the oldest of the brown rabbits took a step forward, wriggled her nose in a critical way, and continued to stare at Sultan.

" Too big ! " she said in a decided voice.

" Too white ! " remarked a rabbit just behind her.

" Too fluffy ! " added a third.

Hardly able to believe his ears, Sultan gazed back at them. How dared they ? How dared these dull, ordinary little brown rabbits criticize *him*, Sultan, the prize Angora, champion at *any* Show ?

He was just going to tell them exactly what he thought about it all when out of the stillness of the wood came the familiar sound of footsteps—footsteps like those of Jane and Henry bringing his supper to the Shed. So these rabbits had not had their supper yet ! This must be somebody bringing their food. Good ! Sultan was hungry again after his adventure, and a nice fresh lettuce leaf, or perhaps some bran and oats, would be most refreshing. Food first—he could deal with these ignorant rabbits afterwards.

Sultan loped a couple of steps towards the approaching sound, then, coming down the path which wound its way between the trees, he saw a man—a queer-looking man—not in the least like Jane—not a bit like Henry !

The man carried no pail of food, but in his hand was
something long and pointed, and it was the sight of this
which, for some strange reason, sent a queer shiver down
Sultan's back.　He felt glad the other rabbits were there.
He looked round, blinked his eyes, and looked round
again.　What *had* happened ?　A moment ago the wood
had been alive with rabbits—rabbits all round him—
rabbits behind every tree.　They had not made a sound,
not a scuffle, not a cry, but now there was not a rabbit
to be seen.

"Come here, Sultan !　Come quickly !　Poacher ! "

For the second time that evening Bobbin's voice
called to him from the mouth of the Warren, and this
time it sounded so urgent, so terrified, that Sultan turned
to follow it without a moment's hesitation.

Pop !　Pop !　Pop !

Something whizzed past Sultan's ear.　Something
buried itself in the ground by his side.　Suddenly panic-
stricken, Sultan ran for his life, and never stopped even
when he reached the mouth of the Warren, but ran on
and on, pushing and struggling down the dark and
narrow passage.

"Well, of all the foolish, ignorant rabbits . . ."

Sultan stopped at last, gasping for breath.　He had
reached the centre of the Warren, and there all the rabbits
of the wood seemed to be sitting waiting for him.

"Don't you know a Poacher when you see one ? "

"I . . . I . . . . thought he was bringing our

supper . . ." muttered the unhappy rabbit. He didn't
feel at all dignified now.

" He was looking for *his* supper," explained the
nearest rabbit.

" He wanted to shoot you," said another.

" And cook you," added a third.

" And have *you* for supper," said yet another brown
rabbit.

" If you can't look after yourself better than that,"
said the oldest rabbit sternly, " you'd better go home."

" I . . . I . . . don't . . ." began Sultan unhappily.

" Don't *what* ? " snapped the old rabbit.

" I don't go home. I mean, I haven't got one now."

" Then you'd better come back and live with me for
a bit," said Bobbin, and without waiting for an answer
he turned and hurried away. Still frightened, still dazed,
and still feeling rather foolish, Sultan followed him
meekly down the tunnel.

CHAPTER III

" ALL wise rabbits sleep in the afternoon."

So Bobbin said, and so Bobbin did, and Sultan, since he had come to live in the Warren, found that it was an excellent habit. He was usually the first to wake, but this evening, as he opened his eyes and gave a long, leisurely yawn, he became aware of a curiously familiar sound near by, which he vaguely connected with the hated preparations for a Show.

" Whatever are you doing ? "

Sultan was wide awake now, sitting straight up and watching with surprised pink eyes as Bobbin systematically groomed his short, brown, fur coat until he was shining and sleek from nose to tail.

" Getting ready for the party," replied Bobbin. " Aren't you coming ? "

" I haven't been invited," answered Sultan.

" Of course you're invited, silly ! *All* the rabbits in the Warren are invited. It's Great Aunt's party, and she never leaves anybody out."

Forgetting all about the dignity expected of a prize

14

Angora, Sultan skipped in the air with excitement, and ten minutes later he was hurrying with Bobbin and several other rabbits along one of the many paths which led from the back door of the Warren up the hill by the wood.

" Where are we going ? " he asked eagerly.

" The Allotment Gardens on the top of the cliff," explained Bobbin. " Great Aunt found a huge bed full of cabbage plants there yesterday, so she thought it would be a good place for a party. She gives the best parties we have, as a rule. Here we are ! Now come and say ' How do you do ! ' "

There were plenty of rabbits about now, all hurrying along the paths which led to the Allotment Gardens on the top of the cliff. At the gate, greeting the rabbits as they arrived, stood the oldest rabbit of all, and Sultan remembered her at once as the first to speak to him in the wood on the evening of his arrival at the Warren.

Great Aunt seemed pleased to see him.

" Still here ! " she said pleasantly. " Go along in. Plenty of cabbages for all ! "

Sultan and Bobbin quickly pushed their way under the gate and joined the crowd of excited rabbits who hurried from cabbage to cabbage, taking a bite here, a nibble there, undecided which plant to choose.

" Here's a lovely one ! "

" Come here ! This is much more juicy ! "

Gaily the rabbits ran to and fro over the loose brown earth. Sultan enjoyed every moment of it—the excitement, the bustle, the hundreds of other rabbits with which to play—but as for the cabbages themselves, he did not think much of them. They were no better than the leaves Jane and Henry brought him almost every day —many of them not as good—and as one by one the other rabbits settled down to supper Sultan wandered away looking for a cabbage that was really worth his while. He found one at last—right at the end of a row —young, green, and tender, sheltered by a tuft of long grass.

Without wasting any more time Sultan scrambled up the tuft towards his chosen supper.

"Look out! Look where you're going! Come back! Sultan, come back!"

Great Aunt was the first to call. At her cry every rabbit stopped eating, and a chorus of frightened rabbit voices shouted out a warning.

"Come back, Sultan! Be careful! Look out! The cliff!"

But it was too late. Even as they spoke Sultan felt the ground crumble beneath his weight. His claws clutched wildly at the slipping earth. Too late did he realize that his tuft of grass, instead of covering a mound of earth as he had thought, had grown away from its roots, and now overhung the steep precipice. The next moment, before the horrified eyes of all the other rabbits, Sultan, cabbage, tuft, and all, disappeared over the edge of the cliff.

Sultan disappeared over the edge of the cliff.

Down, down, down! Crashing, bumping, banging, for what seemed an endless age, the terrified rabbit rolled down the sloping face of the cliff. Bramble branches scratched him as he passed by, snatching tufts of fur from his coat. Spiky rocks jutted out and hit him, and still he fell on, and on, and on.

Suddenly, when he had ceased to think or hope for anything at all, there was a tremendous thud, and all was quiet. Sultan lay for a few moments, dazed and still, then, still very frightened, he raised his head and slowly scrambled to his feet. Yes, he was alive. It was most surprising, but he still had four legs and they all worked properly! In fact, apart from being badly shaken and bruised all over, he seemed none the worse for his fall.

Looking round he found he had fallen upon a stretch of hard sand several hundred feet below the Allotment Gardens and Great Aunt's party. The sight of the high cliff behind him, towering up towards the sky, made him turn quickly away. Beyond the sand he could see water —an unbelievable amount of water—rolling softly to and fro and roaring at him in a most uncomfortable manner.

Miserably Sultan loped along the sand, only to be brought up almost at once by another wall of cliff. Again he tried, but with the same result—in front of him was the sea: behind, and at each side, the towering cliff, too steep for any one to climb. What was a rabbit to do?

Sultan sat down on the driest patch of sand he could

find, to try to think. He had not been there many
minutes when a low wave of water ran towards him,
almost wetting his feet. Then, and not till then, did he
realize the full extent of his danger. The water was not
only roaring at him—*it was chasing him up the beach !* If
it went on like this much longer there'd be no sand left
at all, and *then* what would he do ?

" Hallo ! What are you doing there ? "

The voice came from the direction of the water, and
a face slowly raised itself out of a wave and looked at
him. It was a round face, a queer face, almost an ugly
face, but never had Sultan been so pleased to see anything in all his life before. Talking so fast that his words
fell over each other in their haste to escape from his mouth,
Sultan told the strange and friendly face just what he
was doing there : how he had come, how the water was
trying to chase him up the cliff, and how very much he
wanted to be somewhere else instead.

" Yes, the tide's coming in," was the reply. " There
won't be any sand left in half an hour. My name's Kit,
by the way," and springing easily over a wave a young
Otter landed on the sand and proceeded to shake himself dry.

" I should think the best thing for you to do," Kit
went on, looking round the small cove, " would be to
swim round the corner. There's a path up the cliff there,
and you'd be able to get to the top that way. Come
along ! I'll show you where it is."

He was just going to step back into the water when he noticed the expression of horror on the rabbit's face.

"What, *swim*? In that wet water! *Me*?"

Never had any rabbit looked so wretched. A Show was *nothing* in comparison with this.

"What's the matter? Don't you want to?" asked the Otter.

"I . . . I . . . I can't swim," stuttered Sultan.

"I'll soon teach you," said the Otter. If only he wouldn't be so cheerful about it Sultan felt he wouldn't have minded so much. As it was, shaken and bruised by his fall, the idea of being taught to swim was more than he could bear. Sultan, the prize Angora, the most dignified rabbit in the Shed, burst into tears.

"I'm . . . not . . . going . . . into . . . that cold, wet water!" he sobbed.

"As you like," said the Otter, still cheerful, still smiling. "It will be all right when the tide goes down. You'll be able to walk round then."

"B . . . b . . . but what will I do *now*, when the water comes up to the cliff?" cried the unhappy rabbit.

"You'd better come home with me for a bit," said the Otter. "I've got a cave in this bay that I'm staying in for the present. Come along! There! Isn't that well hidden? Nobody would guess that was the mouth of a cave, would they?"

Proudly the young Otter led the way through a narrow opening between two rocks and into a small cavern in the cliff. It was cold inside, dark, and rather wet. At any other time Sultan would have thought it a disagreeable place, but now it seemed to him the most wonderful spot he had ever seen, and he began to feel better almost at once.

Kit told him to make himself comfortable, and then

began to talk, telling the astonished rabbit of all the wonderful places he had visited—such tales of adventure and narrow escapes that made Sultan's fall down the cliff seem nothing but the most ordinary and everyday affair. So interested did he become that when the Otter said that the tide would have gone down, and that now was the time to make their way round to the cliff path, he felt that he'd have liked to stay for many hours longer.

Together they squeezed through the narrow opening to the cave, and found themselves, to Sultan's astonishment, in a large bay. A long stretch of sand lay before them, while in the distance, glistening in the moonlight, they could see the small wavelets rolling idly to and fro.

"Good! Full moon! We'll find the path easily. Let's race!"

Along the hard sand, side by side, the Otter and the prize Angora ran and ran till they had passed the small headland and came at last to the foot of a narrow path which wound its way up the sloping face of the cliff.

"There it is! You'll find it's quite easy. Rabbits often come down here. Good-bye!"

The Otter nodded, hurried off to a tall rock, and then with a cheerful wave he dived suddenly into the sparkling sea.

Left to himself Sultan started to make his way up the narrow path. "Quite easy" was not at all the way he would have described it. Sometimes it overhung the cliff, often it was slippery, and more than once the white rabbit almost missed his footing and fell again down the steep and terrible precipice. But he reached the top at last and found himself in a field just below the Allotment Gardens.

The moon had long since disappeared, and the first rays of the sun were already showing over the hilltops as Sultan hurried back across the fields. He found his way by one of the many paths which led straight back to the mouth of the Warren. Down the tunnel he hurried— fortunately none of the other rabbits were about—he did not want to stop or speak to anybody. Quietly he crept past Bobbin's doorway, on up the other passages which led to the opening on the railway bank. It was daylight by the time he at last emerged, but Sultan hurried on. Freedom and Adventure were all very well in their way, but what with Poachers, cliffs and one thing and another Sultan was now quite sure that they were as nothing compared with the safety and peace of life in the Shed. His mind was made up. Sultan was going home.

Quickly he made his way across the cornfield, and less than half an hour later he was in the garden, hurrying towards the Shed. Soon he would be safe—his terrors would be at an end, and he would be telling the story of his adventures to an awe-stricken and admiring Shed full of rabbits—rabbits who knew how to appreciate a prize Angora when they saw one.

Quickly Sultan loped down the path : eagerly he hurried up to the door. Then he stopped and gazed blankly before him. *The door of the Shed was closed and tightly fastened !* Wildly he scratched at it with his paw : frantically he bit at the hard wood. The next moment he heard a bark, and Bounce—Bounce the Terrier, on whom he had often looked down with such contempt from the safety of his hutch—bounded out

from behind a bush. Terrified, waiting for nothing more, his last hope gone, Sultan, the prize Angora, turned and rushed away down the path, through the cornfield, till at last he came again to the railway bank, and so to the mouth of the Warren.

It was late in the day when at last he reached the door of Bobbin's home. Bobbin himself was fast asleep, and, treading quietly so that he should not wake him, Sultan crept in and lay down beside the small brown rabbit, closing his eyes at last, after the most eventful night he had known in all his life.

CHAPTER IV

IN THE QUARRY

" You really must learn to look after yourself better ! "

Great Aunt was speaking. She had called to hear how Sultan had escaped from the perils of the cliff, and as she spoke she looked up sternly at the frightened white rabbit before her.

" Ignorant, you are—just ignorant—and, I'm afraid, rather stupid ! Look at the way you rolled down the railway bank : look how you tumbled over the edge of the cliff : look at the silly way you walked right up to that Poacher. Why, the youngest rabbit in the Warren would know better than that ! "

Sultan looked uncomfortably from side to side, afraid to meet the eyes of the indignant brown rabbit, who was little more than half his size. Before he came to the Warren he had been looked up to—admired. All the rabbits he had met at Shows had considered him a fine fellow, a handsome rabbit, and treated him as such ; but here he could do nothing right, and in spite of his size the other rabbits were most condescending.

" We don't wish to be inhospitable," went on Great

Aunt, in a rather kinder voice, " but if you want to go on living in the Warren you really must learn some of the more obvious rules for looking after yourself, or we shall have all the younger rabbits breaking loose and thinking that there's no danger anywhere. Bobbin will teach you. *He* is a sensible rabbit ! "

With these words the angry old rabbit swept out of Bobbin's home and was soon swallowed up in the darkness of the passage.

" Never mind, Sultan," said Bobbin kindly, as soon as she was out of sight. " Great Aunt's much nicer than she sounds, you know, and she is really a very good head to the Warren."

But Sultan did mind—he minded very much. " If you want to go on living in the Warren," Great Aunt had said. He *didn't* want to ; but with the door of the Shed firmly shut, and Bounce ready to leap out at one from behind a bush at any moment, there was nowhere else for him to go.

" It's no good sitting there moping all day," said Bobbin at last. " Let's go out and have a game of hide-and-seek or something."

Sultan didn't mind what he did—he was a miserable rabbit, and everything was horrid — so he followed Bobbin out into the wood ; but when they happened to meet Skurry and Scuttle and several other rabbits, who all agreed that it was just the evening for a game, Sultan began to feel better.

" Let's go to the Quarry ! " suggested Scuttle. " It's a lovely place for hide-and-seek."

Sultan had never been to the Quarry, and when they arrived there and he saw all the interesting little paths running up and down he forgot about being miserable and began to enjoy himself as much as any rabbit there.

He hid behind tree-stumps, he hid in crevices in the rock, he hid among the boulders, and when at last Skurry caught him within a few feet of " home " he was quite ready to take his turn at " finding."

" You and Bobbin are both ' he ' now," cried Scuttle. " Shut your eyes and don't come till we call ' ready.' "

" What a long time they are ! " said Bobbin at last, as, eyes tightly shut, they crouched side by side, half way up the Quarry bank.

" Perhaps we can't hear their voices down here. I'll just go up to the top of the bank and listen."

He was half way up, running lightly over the loose pebbles, when suddenly there seemed to come, from deep down in the Quarry itself, a low rumbling noise, a frightening sound, like the smothered roar of some great monster buried deep below the bank on which he stood.

Ears alert, every hair bristling with sudden terror, Sultan stood still and listened. The moment he stopped running he realized that the whole bank he was on was very slowly, very gradually, beginning to move downwards. Several feet away, across a deep chasm, was a less steeply sloping bank covered with grass and looking

safe and inviting. For once Sultan did the right thing.
Without stopping to think, the moment that he realized
that the slope he stood upon was moving, he took a
tremendous leap, jumping with all the power in his
strong hind legs.   Over the deep chasm he leapt—claws
outstretched to safety—and at last, landing with a thud,
he was thankful to find himself on the firm ground of
the soft grassy bank.

Sultan had not leapt a moment too soon.   Even as
he landed the low rumble increased to a roar, and turning
round he was just in time to see the whole bank, now
nothing but a jumble of roots and stones, heave itself
into the chasm.

Ears back, eyes wide with alarm, Sultan watched the
stones and earth rattle down—for a few moments only,
and then all was quiet, all was still as before.   Except for
an ugly gash in the side of the Quarry, which now cut
straight down at that side in a steep precipice from the
roots of the trees above, the land-slide might never have
happened.

For a moment Sultan could think of nothing but his
wonderful escape, then suddenly, with a gasp of horror,
he remembered Bobbin.   Where was Bobbin now?
When Sultan left him he had been half way down the
slope—the slope that was now nothing more than a
shapeless mound at the foot of the Quarry.

Down the grassy bank as fast as he could go ran
Sultan, till he reached the bottom of the Quarry.   There

was not a moment to lose. Somewhere in that mound
was Bobbin—and Bobbin must be dug out without a
second's delay. Judging roughly where his friend was
most likely to be Sultan started digging frantically.

Faster — faster — faster ! Showers of pebbles and
loosened earth flew out on all sides of him. Never had
Sultan worked so hard—never had he dug so frantically.
But it was no good : hurry as he would the hole in the
earth grew very slowly, and any rabbit buried in the
mound must be suffocated long before Sultan could
reach him.

" If only the others were here ! " sobbed Sultan.
" Why don't they stop hiding ? If only they'd come
back ! "

To go and hunt for them would waste so many
precious moments—it would take too long—Sultan dug
on and on. No ! It was no good ! He *must* have help.
Sultan stopped and looked wildly round. If he couldn't
find the other rabbits there must be somebody about.
He turned and ran rapidly up the grassy bank the way
he had come.

" Help ! Help ! Help ! "

Surely the other rabbits would hear him. But he
was breathless, his voice was weak and the wind was
strong. It swooped down upon him and whirled his
feeble cries up and away into the sky beyond the tops of
the tallest trees.

" Help ! Help ! Help ! "

Somebody was coming! Something moved behind a tuft of heather near by. Sultan rushed towards it at the same moment as a full-grown Stoat stepped out from among the heather.

Sultan had never seen a Stoat before—there had never been anything at all like him at any of the Shows—and without a moment's hesitation he gasped out his story.

" Do come — do come quickly! " he sobbed. " There's been a land-slide, and my friend Bobbin— another rabbit—has got buried, and I want somebody to help me dig him out."

The Stoat looked at him queerly, an evil, hungry glisten in his small bright eyes.

" *Another* rabbit, did you say ? " he asked.

" Yes, this way ! Do come—please come quickly or he'll be smothered."

" It would be a pity for him to be smothered," agreed the Stoat. He licked his lips thoughtfully and then trotted after the white rabbit, who was already rushing once more down the grassy bank.

So busy had Sultan been that he had failed to notice or even to hear the calls of : "Ready! Ready! Ready!" made repeatedly by Skurry, Scuttle, and the other rabbits in hiding. At last, despairing of ever being " found," they crept back one by one to the edge of the quarry.

" What ever is Sultan doing ? "

" What's happened ? "

" Who's that ? "

" Why, it's Sly, the Stoat ! "

There was a flurry of terror, and the next moment
not so much as a rabbit's whisker could be seen upon
the bank above the quarry.   Under cover of bushes,
rocks, tufts of heather or anything else they could find,
frightened rabbit eyes peered down into the depth below.

It was Scuttle who first realized what had happened.

" There's been a land-slide ! " he whispered. " Look !
All that bank's fallen away since we went to hide.   That
must have been that funny rumbling noise we heard !
They're digging for something.   Do you think Bobbin's
got buried ? "

Bobbin buried ! Bobbin buried ! In frightened
whispers the two words passed round the circle of watching rabbits.

" If only Sly wasn't there ! "

" What's Sultan doing ? Doesn't he know how
dangerous Stoats are ? "

Apparently Sultan did not know.   With no thought
for anything but his buried friend he was scattering the
soil wildly in all directions, while at his side, one gleam-
ing eye on the white rabbit and one on the hole they
were making, Sly Stoat's small paws scratched quickly in
the earth.   He was hungry !   The white rabbit would
make a good meal, but two rabbits would be even better
than one, so let this energetic rabbit dig out the second
course for his meal before he started on the first.   Sly
Stoat chuckled wickedly to himself as he dug.

" If only we could warn him ! " muttered Skurry.

" If only we could do something ! " Scuttle groaned.

"We can't ! We can't ! There's nothing we can do ! "

Fascinated, frightened, the hidden group of rabbits on the top of the quarry watched as Sultan and Sly dug

and dug, and Sly watched Sultan out of the corner of his eye.

"Look ! What's that ? " gasped Sultan suddenly.
" It looks like fur ! "

It did look like fur—very like fur—and a little more furious digging proved it to be, quite unmistakably, the tip of a rabbit's ear. Sly Stoat licked his lips and watched Sultan more carefully than ever.

A little more digging brought a second ear to light, and then, to Sultan's tremendous relief, a smothered cry came from the ground beneath them.

" Help ! Help ! I'm down here ! "

" We've nearly got him ! " sobbed Sultan, his breath coming in short gasps of excitement. " Are you all right, Bobbin ? "

" Yes," said the Stoat, with a wicked smile. " Yes ! We've nearly got him ! "

Quiet now, silent, frightened and miserable the rabbits on the top of the Quarry watched and watched.

" I'm all right ! I'm under a wedge of rock."

Bobbin's voice was clearly audible now. A few more inches of earth to scrape away and he would be free.

Sly stopped digging. Now was the moment for him to act. He crouched down, waiting, ready to spring, first upon the digging white rabbit and then upon the prisoner who must soon emerge from the hole they had been making.

So intent was Sly upon his wicked plan, so busy watching for the exact moment at which he should make his spring, that he failed to notice a small shadow, at first no bigger than a tiny speck in the sky above them. Nearer and nearer drew the speck—lower and lower it flew, until a large Kestrel Hawk was clearly visible hovering over the Quarry. Although spotted in places with the soil in which he was digging, Sultan's coat, dazzling in its whiteness, showed up clearly against the brown earth, and it was this that had first attracted the notice of the passing Hawk.

Hovering, dropping gradually nearer, the Hawk made a sudden lightning dive. The next moment his long sharp claws sank deeply into the fur of the unsuspecting white rabbit.

Then everything seemed to happen at once. With a startled screech of fear Sultan struggled and kicked. Bobbin, pushing desperately, at last freed himself from the clinging earth. Sly, furious at the thought that he might, even now, be deprived of his well-planned meal, leapt savagely towards the Hawk. The bird, completely taken by surprise by the sudden attack, loosened his grip sufficiently for Sultan to wrench himself free.

Crying out: "Run, Sultan, run! Run for your life!" Bobbin dashed away, zig-zagging up the grassy bank, and Sultan, too frightened, too dazed to know what was happening, obeyed blindly and rushed after him.

A moment later they had both joined the group of excited, cheering rabbits on the top of the bank.

While down below, in the bottom of the Quarry, a fierce battle raged between Sly and the savage Hawk, the rabbits all together made their way, hidden by the heather and the undergrowth, back to the safety and shelter of the Warren.

"That, Sultan," said Bobbin solemnly, as soon as

Everything seemed to happen at once.

they dared stop for breath, " that was the bravest deed
I have ever seen."

" And fancy thinking of getting a Stoat to help ! "
added Skurry. " A bit risky, *I* think, but very brave
of Sultan."

Sultan didn't understand. All this talk about bravery
was so confusing. He seemed to have become a hero
all of a sudden—a rabbit of importance as he had always
been in the Shed. He couldn't understand it at all.
But Bobbin was safe—he had wanted so much to save
his small brown friend—so everything was all right, and
it really was very pleasant to be a rabbit that mattered
once again.

" Let's go and tell Great Aunt ! " said Scuttle.

Tired, foot-sore, but very happy and contented, and
surrounded by a crowd of cheering rabbits, Sultan made
his way back into the Warren.

CHAPTER V

WHITE RABBIT—BROWN RABBIT

"Sultan! Sultan! Where are you? Great Aunt wants to see you!"

It was no good pretending not to hear. Sultan did not like Great Aunt—he was afraid of Great Aunt—but now all the rabbits in the Warren seemed to be looking for him, and one of them would be bound to find him soon. With as much dignity as he could muster—and he had lost a lot since he came to the Warren—Sultan, the prize Angora, stepped out of Bobbin's house into the tunnel.

He found Great Aunt seated on a mound of earth outside the mouth of the Warren, surrounded by the usual group of young rabbits, all willing and anxious to run hither and thither carrying out the old rabbit's slightest wish.

Great Aunt inclined her head graciously as the white rabbit approached.

"Well done, Sultan," she said solemnly, and then, to his surprise and relief, the old rabbit made a short speech of congratulation for what she called his "bravery and presence of mind in saving one of our number from a horrible end."

"We are pleased to have you among us, Sultan," she said, "and there is only one thing lacking before we can welcome you as a full and honoured member of our community—we do not like your colour!"

For a moment Sultan could hardly believe his long, pointed ears. She—a little brown rabbit who had never even won an "Honourably Mentioned" certificate at any Show—did not like his colour, his beautiful, dazzling whiteness of which he had always been so proud!

"Your colour must be changed!" said Great Aunt decidedly.

"B . . . b . . . but . . ." stammered Sultan.

"It is not only loud and obvious," continued the old rabbit as though he had never spoken, "but it is a danger both to yourself and to your companions. As it is you can be seen wherever you are from a great distance—any enemy could pick you out easily. When you are brown as we are you will be able to conceal yourself in the under-growth, well hidden from the prying eyes of Foxes, Stoats, Hawks, Men, to mention but a few of the evils which abound."

"But I don't know how . . ."

Again Sultan was interrupted.

"We have arranged all that," said Great Aunt kindly. "At the bottom of the wood is a pond, a muddy pond, in fact a pond made up almost entirely of soft, brown

mud and water.   Into this pond you shall be dipped and
well rolled.   You will then come out as brown as any
rabbit could wish.   We will see to the dipping ourselves.
Please be there at six o'clock this evening."

With a nod the old rabbit dismissed him and turned
to talk to one of the young rabbits by her side.

For a moment Sultan stood still, gaping with disgust
at the horrible plan.   Then he turned and ran.   He
wanted to get away—right away.   If only he knew where
to go !   If only the door of the Shed had been left open !
But it was no good trying that.   It was sure to be shut,
and with Bounce about it would be most unsafe to go
and look.   He had learnt enough in the last week to
realize that it would be very dangerous to roam about
the country by himself.   No, there was no escape—there
was nowhere to go.   Sadly he turned his steps in the
direction of the Warren and crept back into Bobbin's
house.

" Hallo !   There you are !   I've got a splendid
idea ! "

Bobbin was in the best of spirits, and so full of his
own affairs that he never even noticed the dejected droop
of the white Angora's ears.

" This house isn't big enough ! " he went on en-
thusiastically.   " It did very well for me by myself, but
now there are two of us it is altogether too small.   My
idea is that we should enlarge it—dig out another room
behind."

A small heap of soft earth in one corner of the room showed that Bobbin had already started work.

" This is just the right time to do it," went on Bobbin. " The earth is so soft after all the rain we've had. Don't tell anybody about the plan, will you ? It's a secret. I shan't let any of the rabbits know till the room's finished, and then I can show it to them all."

" Let me help you ! " said Sultan suddenly.

All the time Bobbin was talking he had been thinking hard. At first he had meant to ask Bobbin to help him escape from Great Aunt's horrible scheme. Then he realized that would be no use. Bobbin was just the same as all the others—he would never have acted against Great Aunt's wishes. Then suddenly the idea had come to Sultan. If Bobbin was going to build a second room and not tell anybody about it, that would be the very place for Sultan to hide in that evening when Great Aunt expected him to be at the pond ! But would the room be big enough by six o'clock to conceal a whole white rabbit ?

" I'll help you ! Let's go on at once ! " said Sultan eagerly.

Bobbin was delighted with the way Sultan had fallen in with his plan, and together they set to work without a moment's delay.

All through the day the two rabbits worked side by side. Gradually the pile of earth grew higher and higher in the middle of the room. Sometimes Bobbin would

stop digging, gather up as much earth as he could carry,
and run with it to the mouth of the Warren, there to
scatter it under the trees of the wood. By the time the
afternoon came Sultan realized, with a sigh of relief, that
quite a big cavern had been dug in the wall, one that

would easily cover him, one in which he would never be
found if he crouched down in the farthest dark corner.

"Poof! I'm tired!"

During the morning and afternoon the two rabbits
had dug vigorously, and now Bobbin felt that he had
had about enough for one day.

"Let's stop now," he suggested. "We can start
again first thing to-morrow morning."

This would never do. It was still quite early in the evening, and if they stopped now and went out, as Bobbin would be sure to want to do, then Sultan felt there would be no escaping Great Aunt at six o'clock.

" I'm not a bit tired," said Sultan firmly. " Surely you don't want to stop yet, do you ? "

Bobbin hesitated. He wanted to get on with the work. He wanted to get his new room finished. If Sultan could go on, then it seemed a pity to give up.

" Perhaps not," he said, and went back once more to the task of scraping and scratching in the soft mud.

For a few moments they worked, then Bobbin stopped again. He *was* tired, it was no good pretending he wasn't—and any way there was all to-morrow, and all the next day, and all the day after that.

" I'm going up for some fresh air," he said firmly. " If you're sensible you'll come too."

But that was exactly what Sultan did *not* want to do. He shook his head, and then, as soon as Bobbin had gone, he hurriedly began to move some of the pile of loosened earth in front of the gap in the wall which led into the new cavern, the better to conceal his hiding-place.

" Sultan ! Sultan ! Sultan ! "

Bobbin had not been away more than five minutes when the white rabbit heard his footsteps come hurrying back along the tunnel.

" Sultan ! Do come ! You'll have to stop now.

Great Aunt wants you, and all the rabbits have been hunting for you for ages."

Sultan stood still, looking miserably down at his friend. Of course this would happen! He had forgotten that Bobbin would be sure to go out, and then, all unknowingly, give him away to the others.

" I can't come ! " he said crossly.   " I'm very tired. I don't feel well."

" Oh, that's all right ! " answered Bobbin cheerfully.   " It's just fresh air you want. I felt like that myself a few moments ago, but it went as soon as I got into the air.   And anyway you'll have to come—it's Great Aunt, you know !   Come quickly—you're awfully untidy, but it can't be helped.   The others are coming to look for you, and if you don't come they'll see this pile of earth and it'll spoil our secret ! "

It was no good.   Sultan's plan had failed.   Sultan would have to go.   Reluctantly he followed his friend along the tunnel, to be met at the mouth of the Warren by numbers of rabbits who crowded round him and began hurrying and bustling him off towards the pond at the bottom of the wood.

" Come along ! "

" Hurry up ! "

" We mustn't keep Great Aunt waiting."

Quickly the other rabbits hustled him along, and it seemed no time at all before they were in the wood and hurrying down the hill towards the pond.

As usual Great Aunt had found a raised mound of
earth, this time close by the side of the pond, and had
seated herself firmly on the top of it. She was looking
about her a little impatiently as the rabbits hurried
Sultan through the trees.

"Ah, Sultan ! There you are ! "

Sultan felt himself pushed and jostled until at last,
shaking in every limb, he was allowed to stop at the foot
of the mound on which Great Aunt sat, and within a
couple of inches of the water itself.

"A little late ! " said Great Aunt, frowning. " A
little late, but—why, what has happened ? "

For a moment the old rabbit stared down at Sultan
with wide, surprised eyes.

"Well done, Sultan," she said solemnly at last. " I
see you have taken our advice. I see you have no need
of our help. We must congratulate you—a good colour—
an excellent colour. We are pleased to welcome you as
a member of the Warren. The pond will not be needed
after all."

With a nod of dismissal to the astonished Angora
Great Aunt turned away from the pond, and, surrounded
by a group of young rabbits, made her way slowly up
the hill through the wood.

What did she mean ? What had happened ? For a
moment Sultan gazed around him, a mystified and bewildered rabbit. Then it was that he caught sight of a
reflection in the water just below him—his own reflection

—and yet was it his own ? Slowly Sultan wagged each of his long ears in turn. Yes, the reflection in the pond waved its ears back at him in faithful repetition. The large rabbit he could see in the water was himself without any shadow of doubt, and yet. . . . Then suddenly he understood. The soft brown earth in which he had been digging, moistened by the recent rain, had discoloured his coat, working its way into his fur until now he was as brown as any rabbit there ! With a sigh of tremendous relief Sultan too turned his back upon the slimy water of the pond.

CHAPTER VI

WORKING IN SHIFTS

" Let's have a rest ! " said Sultan suddenly.

It was three days now since he and Bobbin had started digging the new room for Bobbin's house. They had worked hard, stopping only for meal times and sleeping, and now Sultan was beginning to feel that a whole morning off would be a very good idea indeed.

" We ought to get it finished," said Bobbin doubtfully. " You have a rest if you like. Or, I know! Let's work in shifts."

"Yes, let's!" answered Sultan. He didn't know quite what it meant, but it sounded an important and business-like thing to do. " ' Shifts ' means moving, doesn't it ? " he asked carelessly.

" Not at all," said Bobbin. " ' Shifts ' means that I work this morning and you go out, and then you dig this afternoon while I have a rest—so that there's somebody digging all the time."

Sultan was surprised. He had felt so sure that shifts had something to do with moving, but anyway he thought it was an excellent idea.

" You go first," said Bobbin, " 'cos it's my house.
And anyway I want to finish this bit."

He turned again to the cavern and tiny clods of the
soft brown earth began to fly out behind him, while
Sultan, delighted by the idea of a holiday, scampered
away along the tunnel.

He chose the doorway which led out into the wood.
He liked the trees, and he liked the short, stubby under-
growth. It was ten days now since he had first come to
the Warren—ten days so packed with fresh experiences
and in which he had learned so much that Sultan now
felt he was growing wise in the ways of the wild.

" It will be quite safe to go just a little way by myself," said Sultan, and then promptly forgot all about
it, and rambled on through the wood, farther and farther
from the entrance to the tunnel, on and on, away from
the safety of the Warren.

It was fun exploring: fun to stop work and wander
through the wood. Here and there the bright morning
sun shone in between the leaves of the trees, making
patches of light on the pathway before him.

" I'm glad I came by myself," murmured Sultan.
" Scuttle would have made me keep under cover. Skurry
would have told me to be careful all the time. Now I
can do just as I like ! " and Sultan, the prize Angora,
skipped high in the air, over and over again, with the
sheer joy of a fine June morning.

" Yes, I'm glad . . ." Sultan was beginning again,

but he stopped suddenly on the way to exploring the roots of a most inviting bush. Something, part of the bush he supposed, had twisted itself round his face, and Sultan shook his head vigorously. Bother! The silly thing wouldn't go! Sultan shook his head again, and then, as that made no difference, he started to back out the way he had come.

What was the matter? There was something behind him now—something clutching and clinging that prevented him from making his way out of the bush. There it was, beside him—to right of him—to left of him. Suddenly, with an uncomfortable feeling of distrust, Sultan realized that he was surrounded by small strands of rope, all joined together, which hampered his every movement.

Then it was that the word " snare " came to his mind! He remembered tales told in the Warren of the terrors of these hidden nets which closed suddenly upon the unwary, strong enough to hold any rabbit fast however much he might kick and struggle.

The idea was so alarming that Sultan completely lost his head. For one horrible moment he kicked, struggled, pushed, and pulled with all the power in his strong legs. But it was no good. The only difference that it made was to draw the clinging net even more tightly around him. Tired out Sultan stopped, gasping, and tried to think.

It was no use. He could not find any way of escape. There might be some means of getting out of snares, but

if so he didn't know them. Skurry had never mentioned
any. Scuttle had only talked of the danger of getting
into the horrid things. Perhaps if some other rabbit
were about he might be able to suggest a way.

"Help! Help! Help!" shouted Sultan as loudly as
he could.

" Hallo ! What's the matter ? Want a nut ? "

There was a tiny thud on the ground by his side.
Then something hit Sultan on the nose. Then yet
another small brown hazel nut fell just beside his right
paw.

" I don't want a nut ! " cried Sultan. He didn't
know who had spoken, but to offer a rabbit nuts when
he was firmly rolled up in a snare seemed to him most
out of place.

" I can't get out ! " he sobbed. " I'm all laced up !
Help ! Help ! "

" Well, you are in a mess, I must say ! "

A small red Squirrel came hurrying down the trunk
of a tree and stood there looking at him critically.

" You rabbits! " he went on, quite peevishly Sultan
thought. " Why can't you look where you are going?
That snare's as obvious as anything could be, and yet
you must go and walk straight into it. I shall have to
gnaw it through and let you out, I suppose. That'll be
the third time this week—though I must say the others
were only babies. A great big thing like you ought to
have known better."

Without more ado the Squirrel settled down and started gnawing away at a corner of the net with his strong teeth, chattering and scolding all the while.

"Why you can't bite it through yourself I can't think! But you rabbits are all the same—no brain, no courage, no—no resource!"

The last word seemed to please the small red Squirrel, and he repeated it several times in the interval of chewing at the strands of rope. Sultan said nothing at all. He was far too frightened to mind anything the Squirrel might say to him.

"Nearly through!" exclaimed the Squirrel at last. "One more strand and—— Hush! What's that?"

Sultan listened. At first he could hear nothing, and

then from far away beneath the trees came the measured scrunch, scrunch, scrunch of somebody walking through the wood.

"It's the Keeper!" gasped the Squirrel. "He's coming to visit the snare!" and then, silent at last, he gave his whole attention frantically to tearing away the last remaining strand.

Sultan, stiff with terror, listened as the footsteps came nearer and nearer. Surely the Squirrel could never do it in time!

"Done! Now, quick! Go! Go right away!"

Even as he spoke the Squirrel leapt for the trunk of the nearest tree and, like a streak of red lightning, shot up the gnarled trunk and was lost to view in the branches above.

Sultan needed no second warning. He had heard about Keepers—all that he ever wanted to know—from Bobbin. Throwing off the broken strands of the net he ran, dodging in and out among the trees, away from the approaching footsteps.

On and on he ran. Why had he come so far? In his terror he thought the dread footsteps were following him. Would the entrance to the Warren never come?

At last, as he rounded a large tree, a black and welcome hole opened up before him. In he dashed, gasping thankfully, and then, as soon as he had recovered his breath, he trotted on more slowly down the tunnel.

Perhaps he was tired—he supposed that was it—but

the turning to Bobbin's house seemed a very long way off. Then, at last, he saw an opening on the left and, running straight in, he was just going to call out and tell Bobbin of his adventure when suddenly he stopped dead, every hair rising straight up on his back with horror at the sight he saw. For there, before him, was no

Bobbin, no heap of recently dug earth, but a much larger room than he had expected, a much bigger house altogether, and a few inches only away from him, sleeping peacefully, was the largest Fox Sultan had ever seen! In his hurry through the wood Sultan had mistaken for the mouth of the Warren the opening to a Fox's burrow! Sultan knew about foxes. Only too well he could remember the horror of the night in which one had broken into the Shed, causing the most terrific panic in every hutch, until Bounce had appeared suddenly and driven it away. But now there was no Bounce. Sultan was all by himself—alone with the huge creature just before him. The old Fox moved restlessly in his sleep. Sultan leapt in the air with fright, then, turning round, he crept quietly out and back the way he had come.

Silently he went, and the old Fox slept on. All went well until Sultan was nearing the mouth of the burrow, and then suddenly he saw, silhouetted against the light, the figure of Mrs. Fox returning from hunting and entering the tunnel from the wood.

With a gasp of dismay Sultan stood still. Behind him was the sleeping Fox; in front, and rapidly coming nearer, was a Fox very wide awake, and one who, he feared, had already seen him. On his way he had passed several openings, smaller passages leading out of the main tunnel, and down one of these Sultan now rushed. But he had moved too late. Mrs. Fox had already seen that some strange creature was before her. Then followed a most terrible chase, down endless dark passages under the ground. On and on they went, Sultan running blindly down tunnels of which he knew nothing, the old Fox following, running easily over ground which she knew well.

" What is the matter, my dear ? What is all this fuss about ? "

Round a corner rushed Sultan and then stopped

short—gazing straight up into the sleepy, blinking face
of old Barker Fox.

" Well ! Well ! Well ! " said the old Fox. " So this
is our supper ! Did you bring it far, my dear ? "

" Found it here," said Mrs. Fox shortly. She had
just caught them up and was a little out of breath. " It's
quite a surprise. We don't really want it. We've plenty
for supper. It'll have to go into the larder, then we can
have it for dinner to-morrow."

Unresisting and almost silly with fear Sultan allowed
the two large animals to hustle him down the passage
and back into the room in which he had seen Barker Fox
asleep. Through this they took him and then pushed
him into the larder, a small earthy cupboard down a
short passage at the back.

Left alone in the dark cupboard, so small as to allow
him no room to move, Sultan crouched low. No rabbit
could feel really happy in a larder, and the Fox's larder,
with the words " dinner to-morrow " still ringing in his
ears, was the most terrible place in which Sultan had
ever been.

After what seemed to the unhappy rabbit to be endless
ages of silence he thought he heard a noise quite near
him. Probably the Foxes coming to fetch him, thought
Sultan. But it did not sound like Foxes. It was a queer
noise, a scratching noise, and seemed to be near to his
right ear.

Anything was better than the unnatural quiet, and

Sultan was almost glad that the noise continued, growing gradually louder all the time. Scratch, scratch, scratch. Scrabble, scrabble, scrabble. Was it his imagination, or did a little of the earth from the wall fall to the ground by his side ? It was not imagination ! More earth fell, and then more. Gradually a small hole was opening in the wall. Something that looked like a paw came through it. Sultan had already had too many shocks for one day. Shrinking back in terror against the wall he shut his eyes tightly so that he should not see whatever it might be that would come.

"Why, it's Sultan ! "

Never had the white rabbit opened his eyes so quickly. Never had he jumped forward so eagerly, for there, there in the Fox's larder, was Bobbin's voice calling to him through the hole.

"Bobbin ! Help ! Where are you ? "

"I'm still digging, of course," said Bobbin. "But however did you get *there* ? "

As quickly as he could, in a loud and agitated whisper, Sultan told him about the Foxes, and the larder, and dinner to-morrow, and how necessary it was for him to escape at once.

"Quick ! You start digging your side. We'll soon have the hole big enough for you to get through," said Bobbin, scraping at the earth as fast as ever he could.

Now that he had Bobbin to talk to, now that there was a chance of escape, Sultan became as brave as a rabbit

could be.   He dug furiously, and in a very few moments
they had made the hole so large that he could squeeze
his way through, out of the Fox's larder and into the new
room of Bobbin's house.

"Now we'll block it up again," said Bobbin, pausing
only long enough to help his friend through.

They filled in not only the hole, but the entire new
room—all their work of the past few days—for, as Bobbin
said, they could never feel comfortable living so near
to a Fox.

"In fact I think we'll shut up the whole house,"
said Bobbin.   "There's a very nice one empty nearer
the middle of the Warren, and really I don't consider
this a safe home for any rabbit."

So they moved their things out into the passage,
and firmly sealed up the door to Bobbin's old house
before carrying their belongings into the new one he had
chosen.

Backwards and forwards ran Sultan, only too glad to
help, only too thankful for his wonderful escape.   Suddenly he stopped and looked round at Bobbin, who was
just behind him.

"I *was* right ! " he said triumphantly.   "Working in
shifts *did* mean moving after all ! "

CHAPTER VII

SULTAN'S PARTY

" I MET a rabbit yesterday," said Bobbin importantly.

Sultan was not impressed. He wasn't even surprised. There were several hundreds of rabbits living in the Warren, and it was very unusual to go out without meeting one or other of them.

" He came from a Sand Burrow several miles away on the other side of the wood," went on Bobbin, " and he's asked me to go over and spend a whole day with him and see his home."

This was more interesting, but Sultan did hope he wouldn't. Since the terrible day of the snare and the Fox's burrow Sultan had been afraid to go outside the Warren by himself, and if Bobbin was away for a whole day who would there be to look after him ?

" You can come too, if you like," said Bobbin kindly. " I've never been there before, and I'm not sure of the way, so it will be awfully exciting."

Sultan shook his head. Excitement was just what he didn't want. He had had enough of it in the past few days to last him a very long time, and a journey of several miles to a Sand Burrow neither of them had ever seen sounded to him a very dangerous and difficult business. They were lying on a soft grassy bank, basking in the early morning sunshine, and Sultan felt that it was a great pity ever to think of doing anything else.

"Very well," said Bobbin. "You'll be quite safe here. There are plenty of rabbits about. I shouldn't go out of sight of the Warren door if I were you," and getting up he shook himself vigorously. "I'd better be starting," he added. "I'll be back before sundown, I expect."

He shook himself again, gave a friendly nod towards the sleepy white rabbit, and loped away along the bank at a steady, business-like pace.

Left to himself Sultan blinked lazily in the sunshine. For a little longer he lay stretched upon the bank, then, getting up, he looked about to see how best to amuse himself while Bobbin was away.

A little distance off Skurry and Scuttle were busy nibbling the soft green shoots of grass. On the other side of the bank Great Aunt, surrounded by the usual crowd of rabbits, was giving them a lecture on Stoats and Weasels, and how to avoid them. Yes, it certainly seemed safe enough, but Sultan wished that Bobbin hadn't gone.

Suddenly Sultan realized that he was hungry. Some dandelion leaves would be nice, or a crisp young lettuce, or even a despised cabbage, but he didn't know where to find any of these. Half way up the bank, almost hidden by a large bramble bush, Sultan found a tall, delicate plant, a plant which looked most appetizing, a plant which he felt sure would be very nice to eat. Cautiously Sultan nibbled at one of the leaves. It *was* nice to eat—*very* nice—better than anything the white rabbit had tasted since he had left the Shed. Undoubtedly Sultan had found his breakfast. Settling down behind the bramble bush the prize Angora ate without a pause for ten whole minutes.

"Lovely!" said Sultan at last with a contented sigh. It was the best breakfast he had had for a long time. He had finished now—eaten as much as he wanted—and still three leaves remained on the plant.

"Just enough for breakfast to-morrow!" said Sultan to himself, and carefully pushed the leaves farther underneath the bush. "I hope nobody finds them!"

He felt braver now. He almost wished he'd gone with Bobbin, but as he hadn't he looked round for some amusing way of spending the day.

"I know! I'll see if I can find some more of this lovely plant, then Bobbin and I can have it for supper when he comes back."

It was a good idea, and busily the white Angora hunted about the bank, looking behind every bush, in every hollow, for some sign of the plant he had so much enjoyed.

"It must be a very rare plant," said Sultan at last

with a sigh, then, climbing to the top of the bank, he made his way slowly along it, looking sometimes on one side, sometimes on the other. Before very long the bank ended in a hedge and, scrambling to the top of this, Sultan wandered on looking, hunting, exploring every foot of the way. It was not so easy travelling now. Sometimes tree-stumps blocked his way, sometimes there were bushes to be squeezed through, and once a fallen branch over which he had to climb.

After he had passed three fields in this way and was beginning to think he ought to turn back Sultan stopped with a gasp, for there, in a sheltered hollow on his right, he saw not one but many plants looking just like the one he had so enjoyed for breakfast. Tall and gracefully they grew, sufficient not only for himself and Bobbin, but enough to provide the whole Warren full of rabbits with as much supper as they could eat.

"What a place for a party!" gasped Sultan, then he stopped, stood looking down upon the handsome plants, and thought hard. A party! Why not? He had been to several since he first came to the Warren. Surely it was time he gave one in return. The rabbits had been very kind to him. He had realized that only too well during that terrible time when he had been stored away in the Fox's larder. What would have become of him if they had not taken him in and given him a home? True there was the uncomfortable incident of the pond, but that was over, and even though his coat was cleaner

now nobody took any notice of it, and Great Aunt,
having once declared him to be the right colour, showed
no sign of re-opening the unpleasant subject.   Yes, the
rabbits had been very kind to him.   In return he, Sultan,
the prize Angora, would give them a party !

"Better have it soon while the plants are fresh ! "
thought Sultan.   Yes, the sun was strong and there was
no knowing how soon they might not fade.   He would
have it that very evening.   Bobbin had said he would
be back by sundown, so that would be all right.

Full of his exciting scheme Sultan hurried back along
the hedge.   On the bank he found many of the rabbits
from the Warren, and he ran importantly from one to
the other, busy issuing the invitations for his party.

"Yes, we'd love to come," said Skurry.

"Where is it to be ? " asked Scuttle.

Sultan paused.

"That's a secret ! " he said importantly.   "I think
you'd better all meet me on the top of this bank at sundown this evening, and then I can lead you there."

By the time the afternoon came all the rabbits in the
Warren had been invited, and Sultan lay down for his
afternoon sleep full of excitement and feeling very important indeed.

He stayed indoors until it was time to start, waiting
anxiously for Bobbin to arrive.   But no Bobbin came,
and at last, when the sun was already low in the sky, he
felt that he could wait no longer.

Quite a number of rabbits had already gathered on the bank by the time he arrived. Sultan greeted them with all the dignity of a prize Angora, and in his best Show manner asked them if they would be so good as to wait until the entire Warren had assembled.

More and more of his friends hurried from every direction, and a continuous stream of well-groomed brown rabbits flowed from the mouth of the Warren. It was sad that Bobbin was not there—it wouldn't be nearly so much fun without him—but the sun had not yet set and he was sure to arrive before the evening was over.

Punctually at sundown Great Aunt arrived. All the rabbits were now grouped about the bank, and Sultan announced that the moment had come for him to lead them to the scene of the party.

Never since he had left the Shed had Sultan felt so important. Once more, as he had been at the Shows, Sultan was the centre of the crowd. All eyes were turned upon him as, accompanied by Great Aunt and followed by the entire population of the Warren, he proudly led the way along the hedge. Yes, this was how things ought to be. This was the proper position for a prize Angora, champion of many Shows.

"We are all looking forward to your party," said Great Aunt kindly, then, as Sultan at last stopped on the top of the hedge: "Which way is it now?" she asked.

Not very intelligent of the old rabbit, thought Sultan. They were now in sight of his waving mass of plants, and she had not said a word about them. Perhaps she had not noticed, and, turning sharply to the right, Sultan led the way down the side of the hedge. He did not stop until he and Great Aunt were in the very middle of the tempting plants, the other rabbits crowding eagerly round them.

" We have arrived ! " announced Sultan. He was very excited. It *was* a lovely treat for them all ! " Help yourselves ! " he said graciously, then, as no one moved : " This is the—er—feast," he added. " Please begin ! "

Great Aunt looked at him—all the rabbits looked at him—but none of them began to eat.

" Won't you start ? " said Sultan a little nervously.

" Start what ? " asked Great Aunt in an icy voice.

" Start eating ! " answered Sultan. " Look ! Don't you see ! " and he bent a branch of a fresh green plant low before Great Aunt's nose.

Great Aunt said not a word. With a look of tremendous scorn the old rabbit glared at him : then, in dead silence and with dignity bristling every hair, she turned and retraced her steps up the hedge, a pathway opening up before her among the hundreds of rabbits who were crowding down.

Not a rabbit spoke. Not a word was uttered. With looks of the deepest disgust each rabbit turned away. Silently the seething mass of rabbits made its way up the hedge, back along the path to the Warren. In ten minutes there was not a whisker to be seen. Of all that had accepted Sultan's invitation, not a rabbit remained to enjoy the party he had so proudly prepared for them.

What was the matter with them all? What had happened? Never had the white Angora felt so utterly dejected and bewildered. If only Bobbin was there he would be able to explain. But no Bobbin came. Alone

Sultan waited in the gathering darkness, until at last, frightened by the silence, miserable and lonely, he crept back to the Warren, made his way quietly along the tunnel, and hid himself in the shelter of Bobbin's house.

"Hallo! There you are! I've had such a lovely day!"

Bobbin at last! If only he had come before! But even now perhaps he would be able to explain.

Sadly, in short, jumbled sentences, Sultan jerked out the story of his party, and it was some moments before Bobbin could make out exactly what had happened.

" I can't understand it at all," said Bobbin, a puzzled frown on his face, as soon as he had understood what Sultan was trying to tell him. " I think you'd better show me where it happened."

Once more Sultan led the way up the bank and along the hedge, a very different Sultan from the proud rabbit of a few hours before.

"Here we are! This is where it was!" he said at last, and pointed to the plants he had discovered that morning.

" What ? *Those !* "

Bobbin's voice was full of horror as he stared down at the moonlit field.

" Yes ! " said Sultan. " Those ! "

" Why, my good rabbit, that's hemlock ! Don't you know it's poison ? "

Poison ! So that was why ! The rabbits thought he was trying to poison them all. At last Sultan was beginning to understand.

" You haven't eaten any yourself, have you ? " asked Bobbin anxiously.

" Yes ! Of course I have," and Sultan told Bobbin about his breakfast.

" Let's go back ! Let's go and tell the others ! " said his friend nervously. " Do you feel ill ? "

Sultan thought he did—yes, he was almost sure he did—but he could manage to get back to the Warren.

Bobbin's first move was to tell Great Aunt, then to let all the other rabbits know about Sultan's sad mistake. The news spread rapidly through the Warren, and the rabbits, good-natured at heart, came hurrying out of the tunnel, anxious now to offer their sympathy and to tell Sultan that they quite understood.

In a sympathetic group they gathered round, gazing sadly at the frightened Angora.

" How are you ? "

" Do you feel very bad ? "

" You aren't dead yet, are you ? "

" I don't know ! Yes, I think so ! No, I'm not ! "

Sultan, too frightened to know what he was saying, looked miserably round him. He thought he felt ill—he was sure he felt ill—very ill indeed.

" Not dead yet ? Well, I'm sure you ought to be ! " remarked Great Aunt. " Hemlock generally works quicker than this ! "

No, he wasn't ! He didn't think he was, but really he hardly knew.

" Where is this plant you eat ? You'd better show us," Great Aunt snapped out.

Hardly knowing what he did Sultan led the way to the bramble bush and pointed sadly to the few leaves that remained from his breakfast.

Then, for the first and last time in his life, he saw

Great Aunt laugh. She sat down upon the ground and laughed till she rocked. She laughed till her whiskers shook and the bank echoed with the sound. She laughed until the other rabbits, crowding round, lost their anxious looks and laughed as well, and soon the whole bank seethed with shaking, mirthful rabbits.

Sultan grasped at his last remaining shred of dignity. He looked angrily round. If he was poisoned, if he was going to die, he'd like to do it quietly and not among all this noise !

"Oh dear, of all the funny rabbits ! Oh dear ! Oh dear ! "

Then, turning to Sultan, Great Aunt went on: " I

was told it was *hemlock* you'd eaten—hemlock such as you offered us at your party—but this is only cow parsley. It's very like it, but it isn't hemlock! Cow parsley!" once more the old rabbit shook with laughter. "And now you think you feel ill! You funny rabbit! Cow parsley! A most nutritious—a most healthy food!"

For a moment Sultan blinked at her—then he understood. Feeling suddenly much better, but not wanting to meet any of the rabbits for a very long time, he pushed his way through the crowd and hurried back to the Warren.

CHAPTER VIII

FIRE! FIRE! FIRE!

"Fire! fire! fire!"

"Did you call?" asked Bobbin, opening one eye and looking up sleepily. It was early in the afternoon. A few minutes before all the Warren had been silent—rabbits sleeping peacefully in every house—but now suddenly everything was changed. Everywhere was bustle, everywhere excitement, and down the dark tunnel panic-stricken rabbit voices called over and over again the words of warning: "Fire! Fire! Fire!"

"Was'er matter?" Bobbin was very sleepy indeed. "Did you call?"

"Yes! Lots of times! Wake up! Do wake up quickly."

Sultan, himself only just roused from sleep, was wide enough awake to realize that something was happening—something about which Bobbin ought to know. In the tunnel was the sound of many feet running—everywhere the chatter of frightened rabbits. Through the door there stole a faint but unmistakable smell of smoke. Bobbin smelt burning! Bobbin's nose, wriggling in-

quisitively, sniffed the air again. The next moment the
small brown rabbit was awake and on his feet.

" Come on ! " he said. " No time to lose ! We must
go ! Come quickly ! "

As he finished speaking Bobbin was already out of
the door and hurrying down the tunnel.

The smell of smoke in the passage was quite unmistakable. Even Sultan knew what it was. It reminded
him of the bonfires they sometimes had in the garden—
most disagreeable when the wind was the wrong way
and blew the smoke into the Shed. All around them
were rabbits hurrying. Frightened rabbits burst out of
every doorway, all rushing, pushing, and scrambling
towards the nearest opening to the Warren.

Down the tunnel rolls of smoke were blowing, suffocating, choking smoke which made the rabbits all the
more eager to escape from the crowded tunnel. Terrified
—pushing past each other—rabbits rushed hither and
thither. Suddenly through the Warren rang the voice
of Great Aunt.

" Stop ! " shouted the old rabbit, stamping her foot
noisily upon the ground. " Stop ! Not another rabbit
is to leave the Warren ! "

Startled and alarmed they all stood where they were,
listening to the commanding and imperious voice of the
old rabbit as she ordered sentinels to every doorway,
instructing them to see that not a single rabbit passed
through until such time as she should say they might.

" Don't you understand that rushing away is the
worst thing you could do ? " stormed Great Aunt.
" What is to happen to the Warren if every rabbit deserts
it, running away at the first sign of danger ?   Why, the
Warren would be burnt out—and what would you all
do then, I should like to know ?   How would you fare
out in the open—think of Weasels, Foxes, any kind of
danger—if there were no Warren to which you could
run ? "

The old rabbit was getting so excited that her voice
was turning into a shrill scream.   Twice she had to stop,
almost choked by the smoke which was now rolling up
in clouds along the tunnel, but she went on again fiercer,
more determined than ever.

" If the Warren goes you are all doomed rabbits ! "
she shouted.   " Your only hope is to stay here and fight
the fire.   And think of the rabbits that can't go out !
There's Long Ears, who has a cold—and what about
Woolly's babies, who are *much* too young to take out in
the open ? "

Great Aunt paused, and for a moment there was
silence except for the choking of several rabbits, half
suffocated in the smoke.

" Not a rabbit is to leave the Warren," finished up
Great Aunt impressively.   " Your only hope is to stay
and fight the flames."

Shivering with fright, anxious only to escape from
the horrible dark tunnel, Sultan looked around him.   It

was all very well to be told to fight the flames, but if there weren't any flames to fight, only clouds of thick, suffocating smoke rolling down endless yards of dark tunnel and coming from who knew where, he didn't really see what any rabbit could be expected to do about it. Around him frightened rabbits ran aimlessly to and fro. Bobbin had disappeared into the crowd.

It was all too much for Sultan. He didn't know what he ought to be doing. He didn't *care* what he ought to be doing. He knew what he wanted to do—what he was going to do—and that was to get out into the fresh air as quickly as he could.

Every moment the Warren became more and more unbearable. Every moment the smoke grew denser, breathing more difficult. Sultan made off as fast as he could to the nearest doorway out of the Warren.

" No exit ! "

Bother ! He had forgotten Great Aunt's sentries ! Two lusty young rabbits stood firmly in his path, blocking the way to safety.

Back went Sultan, on and on along the tunnel, pushing his way past crowds of rabbits—stupid rabbits—rabbits all waiting there to be suffocated—till he came to another entrance, only to meet with the same result. One by one Sultan tried every exit in turn until only the opening on to the railway bank remained. He had left this till last because it was from here that the smoke seemed to be blowing.

The stretch of tunnel leading to the railway bank, long since deserted by all the other rabbits, was now nothing but a rolling bank of smoke. Even the sentries had been allowed to leave, as Great Aunt considered that the passage was now impassable.

Sultan went slowly towards it. In the distance he

could hear Great Aunt shouting orders at the top of her voice. She was coming nearer. Somewhere a rabbit choked. Suddenly Sultan gave way to panic. Better to make one wild rush through the smoke than to suffocate slowly in this awful underground trap. Sultan turned and rushed frantically towards the doorway leading on to the railway bank.

(3,944)

6

More and more blinding became the smoke. With
every step the passage grew hotter. What Sultan did
not know was that the fire, the cause of all the turmoil,
was smouldering outside on the railway bank—that every
step he took was only leading him nearer and nearer to
the danger from which he was trying to escape. But if
he had known it would have made scarcely any difference.
The white rabbit was far too frightened to think—too
terrified to do anything but run, and run, and run. . . .

One thing only saved Sultan from rushing out and
ending his days in the fire. Early that afternoon a large
red Cow had wandered through a hole in the hedge to
crop the grass upon the railway bank. A few moments
later a train rushed past, so startling the Cow that she
tossed her head, kicked her heels into the air, and raced
madly back up the bank, while a spark from the engine,
lighting on the dried-up grass, smouldered quietly, later
to burst into flame. Not looking where she was going
the Cow trod heavily upon the edge of a large rabbit hole
half way up the slope. She slipped, nearly fell, recovered
herself, and rushed on to the top and into the field from
whence she had come.

But the rabbit hole did not recover. The Cow had
trodden heavily and had broken down the edge, leaving
but a very small gap where the large hole had been.

It was towards this that Sultan now rushed in his
terror. The thicker grew the smoke, the hotter the
passage, the faster ran the panic-stricken white rabbit.

At last he reached the hole and was horrified to see the size of it. Wildly he pushed against the small opening. But it was no good. The clod of earth which the Cow had trodden down stood firmly before him.

"I'll try backwards!" gasped the rabbit to himself. "I can push harder that way."

The smoke was now blinding, the heat intense. Turning his tail towards the opening, his four feet planted firmly on the floor of the tunnel, the white Angora pushed and pushed again with all the strength he could muster.

It was no good. The earth which blocked up the hole stood firm. Again Sultan pushed, and pushed, and pushed. . . .

At last the white rabbit realized that he would have to give it up. The path of escape was completely blocked —there was nothing for him to do but to return as quickly as possible to the cooler, less smoky, parts of the Warren.

It was one thing to think this but quite another to do it. When he tried to move Sultan discovered to his horror that he was tightly wedged in the mouth of the Warren.

With all his remaining strength Sultan kicked and struggled, but all to no avail. He had pushed himself so firmly into the narrow opening that now no amount of effort on his part would free him. The heat from the outside was intense, the smoke in the tunnel overpowering.

Suddenly Sultan's struggles came to an end, his feet

ceased to kick against the earth. Worn out by his
efforts, suffocated by the smoke, Sultan, the prize Angora,
had fainted.

. . . .

It was Skurry who discovered him. Rushing to and
fro, telling each other what ought to be done, deciding
how best to fight the fire, the rabbits in the Warren
gradually realized that the smoke was growing less.
Dense clouds no longer rolled down the passage leading
towards the railway bank, and the smoke which had
already come gradually dispersed and spread itself about
the Warren, the greater part of it filtering away through
the other entrances.

At last Great Aunt said it would be safe to explore
the passage, and asked for a volunteer.

" I'll go ! " said Skurry, always ready for an
adventure.

In a few moments he was back again, bristling with
news.

" It's Sultan ! " he gasped. " It's the bravest deed
I've ever seen ! He's wedged himself into the doorway
leading on to the railway bank so that no more smoke
can get in ! "

Shouts and cheers from all the rabbits in the Warren
greeted Skurry's news. Great Aunt sent a scout hurrying out through another entrance and round on to the
railway bank, and before long he was back, announcing
that the fire was out and all was now safe. The fire

had, indeed, died down to a comparatively harmless smoulder almost as soon as Sultan decided to make his dash for safety, or the white rabbit would have been roasted.

Dozens of rabbits now hurried to the spot, some up the tunnel, others out into the open and down the railway bank, and in a very short time they had repaired the damage done by the Cow's hoof, and Sultan was free once more. A little water from the pond soon revived him, and the white rabbit awoke to find himself the hero of the Warren—the gallant rescuer who had saved them all from the fire.

CHAPTER IX

THE COUNTRY HOUSE

" Sultan ! Sultan ! Where are you ? "

The white rabbit looked up at the sound of his name in time to see Scuttle hurrying over the ground towards him. Scuttle was excited—Scuttle had news, and he wanted to tell it just as soon as he could.

" Found you at last ! " he panted. " I've been look-ing everywhere. Bobbin said you'd be just outside."

" I hadn't gone far," said Sultan. " I only . . ."

But Scuttle wasn't interested. He wasn't even listening. He was completely wrapped up in what he had to say, and now broke in eagerly.

" How would you like a holiday by the river ? " he asked. " I've just been talking to Woolly. She has taken a country house for her babies. It's on a hillock down by the river—a beautiful spot she says, and right in the middle of one of the best feeding-grounds around here. She says she's been making ' extensive alterations '—dug it out herself mostly. She says her babies won't be old enough to travel there for at least seven or eight days, and she's offered to lend it to us till then if we like to spend a week there."

Sultan blinked doubtfully. It certainly sounded very nice.

" I've asked Bobbin," went on Scuttle before Sultan had time to say anything at all, " and he thinks it's a lovely idea—just for the four of us—Skurry and me and you and Bobbin."

If Bobbin had said so then it must be all right, and Sultan began to get nearly as enthusiastic as Scuttle over the plan.

" When do we start ? " he asked eagerly.

" Almost now," said Scuttle. " There's nothing to wait for, and the sooner we go the longer we shall have there. Bobbin's just gone to shut up his house."

" I'll soon be back ! " said Sultan, and raced off to help Bobbin, pausing only to nod in agreement to Scuttle's suggestion that they should all meet at the mouth of the Warren in ten minutes' time.

He found Bobbin full of plans for the holiday.

" We'll have a lovely time ! " he said. " I know the river bank well—it's the nicest part round here. There ! I think that's everything now. Come along or the others will be waiting."

It was a hot, sunny day and the four rabbits started off in the best of spirits. The river bank was some distance away and it took them all that was left of the morning and most of the afternoon to reach the hillock on which was Woolly's country home. Scuttle had spoken truly. It was a delightful spot, and all around grew grass of the softest and tenderest—a much finer variety than that which they found near the mouth of the Warren, down-trodden as it was by the feet of many rabbits.

" It's good to get right away from the crowd," said Skurry. " The Warren's all very well in its way, but it *is* nice not to have dozens of rabbits round one *all* the time."

The others agreed, and after resting for a little time in Woolly's house, which they found most comfortable and just the right size for the four of them, they went out for a lovely evening's ramble along the bank of the river.

" I do believe it's going to rain ! " said Bobbin at last. It was sundown, and great black clouds were rolling up from the west, shutting out much of what was left of the daylight.

" It's started already," answered Skurry. " I distinctly felt two drops on the tip of my nose. Come, let's race for home ! "

Together the four rabbits scampered along the river bank and arrived at last at Woolly's house, just as the rain began to fall in steady, even drops. Woolly had dug out her burrow well. Though small there was ample room to shelter the four rabbits from the rain and, tired out but thoroughly happy after a whole day in the open, they settled down and slept soundly through the night.

Sultan was the first to wake. Peering out through the mouth of the burrow he saw to his disgust that the rain was still pouring down. Drops of water dripped from every bush: the earth looked soft and black and the sky heavy, without a break in the dark grey clouds.

" It's been raining all night, I think," he said dismally as Scuttle joined him in the doorway.

" It looks as if it's going to rain all day too," added Scuttle. " It's too bad, just when we've come for a holiday."

It did rain all day, and all the next night, and all the day following that. The four rabbits, growing more and more depressed, amused themselves as well as they could in the restricted space of Woolly's country house, going out only when hunger drove them, and then grabbing at the nearest dandelion leaf or tuft of grass and scampering in again as fast as ever they could.

Drip, drip, drip! Would the rain never stop? They awoke on the third morning to find no clearance in the sky, no hopeful signs that the steady fall of rain would ever break.

" The river's looking awfully fierce! " said Skurry, returning from a rush out after food. " It's risen such a long way, and is all brown and frothy along the edge of the bank."

It certainly was rather an alarming sight, and when

Bobbin went out a few hours later he reported that the river was now so full that it had reached the top of the bank and even bubbled over in one or two places.

It was left to Sultan to make the really frightening discovery. For want of something better to do the four rabbits slept most of that day as well as the night. When the white Angora went out in the evening to grab the best supper he could among the raindrops he was horrified to find that the river had not only overflowed its banks but a steady stream of water was running on the wrong side of the hillock on which Woolly's house was built. A second glance assured him he was right. They were now completely surrounded by water.

" We'll be drowned ! " he said miserably as he told the other rabbits the alarming news. " We'll be drowned ! I know we shall ! Whatever can we do ? "

" There's nothing we can do," said Bobbin. "Not at this time of day anyway. It can't rise much in the night, and perhaps the rain will have stopped by morning."

But the rain had not stopped when they awoke on the following day. It was still pouring steadily down, and what had been a mild stream on the wrong side of the hillock was now a rushing torrent several feet in width.

" We'd better go out and explore and see if there isn't some way by which we can escape," suggested Skurry. " If Bobbin goes up the river bank, and Scuttle down it, I will take the land side. You'd better stay in here and keep dry," he added, turning to Sultan. " I don't expect you'd know the sort of thing to look for."

The three rabbits set out on their scouting expedition, and, left to himself, the white Angora stamped angrily round the house. Why hadn't they taken him with them ? Why had he been left behind ? Of course he'd know what a way of escape looked like just as well as they did. He might have been able to rescue them all ! He *would* rescue them all ! He'd stay in the house just as they had told him and find a way of saving all four of them. He'd dig a tunnel right down through the floor of Woolly's house, underneath the flood and up again, opening on to the safe dry land the other side.

This seemed a wonderful idea to Sultan, and he chuckled with glee as he thought how surprised the other rabbits would be when they saw what he had done. Leaving him behind to keep dry, indeed ! He wouldn't know the sort of thing to look for, wouldn't he ? He'd show them !

Busily Sultan set to work, digging a deep hole straight down in the floor of Woolly's country house. Determined to have the passage well started before the other rabbits returned he wasted not a moment, but dug as fast as ever he could.

" It will have to be a deep hole before I start the passage," muttered the white rabbit to himself, " or it will never get under all that water."

Meanwhile the three rabbits raced along through the rain drops. Up the river hurried Bobbin, down the bank ran Scuttle, while Skurry explored the land side, until they had, between them, been all round the island hillock without finding any hope of escape.

"We shall just have to stay where we are and wait for the rain to finish," said Bobbin, when he met Skurry on the far end of the hillock.

"I hope it stops soon," answered Skurry uncomfortably.

On the way back they met Scuttle, who had nothing better to report, and together the three sodden rabbits made their way sadly back to Woolly's house.

"We shall be able to dry ourselves here, anyway," said Bobbin, then he stopped dead. "Why, Sultan, whatever has happened?"

The three rabbits stood dripping in the doorway, astounded at the sight that met their eyes. In the middle of the house, the nice dry house, shamefaced and alarmed, stood the white rabbit gazing down with horror at a large hole at his feet, a hole from which more and more water was oozing and gradually flowing into all the corners of the room.

"I thought I'd had a good idea," said Sultan, looking up guiltily as he heard the others come in. "I thought I'd dig a tunnel—a way of escape for all of us— and . . . and . . . I don't know why . . . but look what's happened!"

Sultan had dug down to water level, and now Woolly's house, their one hope of shelter, was rapidly becoming filled with water !

" We must get out of here as quickly as we can," said Bobbin, and turned back into the open once again.

The rain was now coming down harder than ever.

Never in all their lives had the rabbits known it go on for so long a time. Rapidly the river was rising on one side of them, the flood on the other. The hillock was growing smaller and smaller, and there was not one among them that did not realize how very dangerous their position was becoming.

" The water's rising quickly. We'd better climb on

to the highest ground we can find," suggested Skurry, and together they clambered up the hillock. Near the top they found a log of wood, a branch which long ago had fallen from a neighbouring tree, and on to this they scrambled as being the spot further from the rising water than any other they could find.

The rain had at last almost stopped, but the river, swollen by the flooded streams which poured into its upper regions, was increasing in force at every moment, and the floods rose rapidly around them. Higher came the water, mounting inch by inch up the hillock until the end of the very log of wood on which the frightened rabbits crouched was in the water. Unknown to them there was yet another danger threatening. Waves of water curled up the side of the wood. The next moment the log, together with its passengers, was afloat on the surging river.

After a first gasp and squeak of terror the four rabbits crouched silently down upon the top of the floating log. In fact talking would have been both difficult and useless, made almost impossible as it was by the rush of the water combined with the roar of the not far distant waterfall. Faster and faster the river carried them along, nearer and nearer to the peril of the waterfall.

Putting his mouth close to Skurry's long ear Bobbin took a deep breath and shouted as loudly as he could.

" The corner ! " he yelled. " The bank juts out at the corner. We may catch on it ! It's our only hope ! "

Faster and faster the river carried them along.

They were floating not many feet away from the right bank of the river. A little way in front of them the river took a sharp turn to the right, leading to the reach which ended in the deadly waterfall. At this corner a ridge of high land jutted out for several feet into the river, and it was here that, as Bobbin had suggested, the log they were on might be delayed for a second or two on its course.

Nearer and nearer they rushed to the jetty of land.

" Get ready to jump ! " howled Skurry.

The others could not hear him, but they knew what he meant, and, crouching lower still upon the log, each rabbit made sure of as firm a foothold as possible from which to spring.

At one moment it seemed as though their boat was to be swirled away into mid-stream before the hoped for landing-stage was reached, but in the nick of time a twig, projecting from the water, turned its course again, this time even nearer to the bank than before.

The log rushed on. They were almost level with the jetty. For a second the front of the log touched the protruding ground.

" *Now !* " yelled Bobbin and Skurry together.

Four rabbits summoned all the courage that was theirs. Four rabbits, every muscle taut, crouched low, then sprang into the air. For a moment, in mid-air, above the roaring water, four rabbits shot through the spray towards safety. The log momentarily disappeared under the water with the force of the mighty leap. Bobbin landed safely upon the bank, and almost simultaneously Skurry arrived at his side. Sultan, paws outstretched, joined them a second later as a cry from Scuttle announced that he was hanging, only half in

safety, his hind legs in peril of dragging the whole of him back into the rushing river.

In a second Bobbin had hold of one of his long ears, while Skurry seized the other. Sultan rushed up and down, making encouraging sounds, and in less than a minute they had hauled him up the bank, and all four rabbits lay panting, sodden with rain and spray, but safe upon the river bank.

"Look at the log!" gasped Bobbin, the first to raise his head.

The others turned towards the river in time to see what had so recently been their boat raise itself on end in the water and then disappear from view over the crashing, foaming waterfall not twenty feet away.

With eyes filled with awe the four rabbits looked at each other, then, squeezing as much water as they could from their dripping coats, they set off silently in the direction of the Warren.

CHAPTER X

THE FALLEN TREE

" If only the wind wouldn't blow so much!" muttered Sultan.

It blew the tall grass till it lay in flat waves about the field of uncut hay. It blew his long white hair the wrong way along his back, parting it in strange places and letting in the cold, which sent little shivers all over him.

But the wind whistled louder than ever in the trees, and Sultan drew closer to the protecting hedge. He was sorry he'd ever come out—wished he'd stayed in the Warren, which was at least warm and still—but he and Bobbin had run out of stores and he was hungry . . .

Crash !

For a moment Sultan stood still, ears pricked, every sense alert—waiting to hear what would come next. But there was no further noise—nothing but the monotonous whining of the wind in the tree tops and rustling of the grass, now hardly noticeable after the deafening, crackling, thud which had seemed to shake the ground under his feet. It came from behind him and, frightened but even more curious, Sultan turned and crept back along the path by which he had come.

"What ever can it have been?" murmured Sultan.

Then suddenly he saw it. An enormous tree—the big elm at the corner of the field under which he had passed less than five minutes ago—now lay crushed and broken

upon the ground. Its branches spread far over the grass, and broken twigs scattered the field for yards around.

"Oh!" gasped the white rabbit.

Four minutes—three minutes earlier and he, Sultan, would have been lying buried underneath the wreckage! Frightened but fascinated by the idea Sultan crept nearer. He stood and gazed at it for a moment, and then was just about to hurry away when he thought he

heard a cry—yes, he was sure he heard a cry—from the
far side of the tree.

The tree seemed even bigger upon the ground than
it had when it stood upon the hedge, and it took Sultan
several minutes to clamber over the spreading roots and
reach the far side.

" Help !   Help ! "

The cry was unmistakable now.   Sultan pushed his
way quickly among the tangle of branches then stopped,
horror stricken at the sight before him—Great Aunt,
peering through a cage of broken twigs, one of her back
legs pinned firmly to the ground by a heavy branch.

" Thought you were never coming ! " said the old
rabbit composedly.   " Here am I, not two fields away
from the mouth of the Warren, and not a rabbit comes
when I call !   Disgraceful ! "

Sultan stood and gaped at her.   Didn't she *know* of
the danger she'd been in ?   Didn't she realize that even
now she was not at all safe ?   As if he had spoken out
loud Great Aunt answered the latter question for him.

" Don't stand staring there ! " she snapped.   " Can't
you see what a helpless state I'm in ?   What are you
going to do about it ?   Something quickly, I hope ! "

What was he going to do ?   What *could* a rabbit do ?
He'd never seen Great Aunt in such an undignified
position before—and she was expecting him to *do* something about it !   It would take many more than one
rabbit to move the bough.   If only Bobbin were here . . .

"Well? Hurry up! If you can't do anything by yourself you'll have to have help . . ."

Help! That was an idea! He'd go back to the Warren and fetch some other rabbits.

"Where are you going?" cried Great Aunt angrily, as he turned away. "What—you surely didn't think you could leave me alone and unprotected in this helpless condition? Why, *anything* might happen! Call, rabbit! Call!"

His pink eyes large and round with confusion Sultan opened his mouth and called "Help! Help! Help!" over and over again in a high, squeaky voice.

But it was no good. No rabbits appeared. It was doubtful whether Sultan's cries could have been heard even on the far side of the tree, and in that roaring wind it was hopeless to try to make his voice carry farther.

"Help! Help! Help!"

There was no answer to his cry. Nobody came.

"Help! Help!"

This time somebody did come. There was a rustling, crunching sound in the hedge just above him. Sultan turned eagerly round, looked up, and saw—a Fox looking down at him! It was a large Fox—the same that Sultan had once visited by mistake in his burrow—and now, standing upon the top of the hedge with the wind ruffling his handsome red coat, he seemed to the frightened rabbit to be a most gigantic creature.

Sultan took one look then, forgetting Great Aunt,

Sultan turned eagerly round . . . and saw a Fox.

forgetting the fallen tree, forgetting everything in the world except the Fox behind him, Sultan turned and ran.

The Fox ran too—after Sultan—over the field, up the hedge and down the other side, every step bringing him nearer to the bobbing white tail before him.

But Sultan had had a good start—the broken branches

had prevented the Fox from jumping easily from the hedge —and the Warren was only two fields away.

On rushed Sultan, across the second field towards the mouth of the Warren, in through the opening, and, gasping for breath, down into the safety of the Warren itself.

For some moments he lay panting in the dark tunnel

then, eager to tell the other rabbits about his adventure with the Fox, he hurried on.

"Bobbin! Bobbin! I've had such a terrible time!"

But Bobbin did not seem interested. He just nodded in a preoccupied way and then turned and went on talking to Scuttle.

"I can't *think* where she can be," he was saying.

Scuttle shook his head, frowning.

"It isn't like Great Aunt to be away from the Warren for a whole morning—especially when she had arranged to give a lecture on 'Traps and Snares, and How to Recognize Them' to the younger rabbits."

Great Aunt . . .! Then Sultan remembered. He ought never to have left her alone and unprotected . . . how could he tell the other rabbits? A shudder of horror ran all the way up his back as he thought of the Fox . . . and Great Aunt . . . alone and helpless. . . .

Somehow he managed to blurt out his story. The other rabbits, all attention the moment he mentioned Great Aunt's name, listened eagerly as he told of the fallen elm tree, the old rabbit's cry for help, the heavy branch that pinned her to the ground. But the rest of his story fell on deaf ears, or rather on vanishing tails, as every rabbit in the Warren turned and scampered away towards the nearest opening—intent upon the rescue of Great Aunt.

"The Fox! The Fox! There's a Fox in the field!" shouted Sultan.

" We'll go by the wood entrance, then," called Scuttle, and every rabbit turned aside and rushed along the tunnel which led to the wood.

In a few moments all was silent. Except for Sultan, not a rabbit remained in the Warren. Old rabbits, young rabbits—all had hurried to the rescue. Left alone Sultan crouched, guilty and uncomfortable, by the door of Bobbin's house. What a coward he'd been! How *could* he have forgotten Great Aunt?

The silence in the deserted Warren made him feel even more miserable. Sadly he crept to the doorway, but there the wind howling round the tops of the trees made him feel more unhappy than ever, and he loped back into the Warren again.

Many minutes later—a great many Sultan thought—he heard a sound of returning rabbits. What had happened to Great Aunt? What were they going to tell him? Sultan shut his eyes and wished very much that he was somewhere else.

The next moment the Warren was full of rabbits—laughing, shouting, talking rabbits—while more poured in through every doorway.

Sultan opened his eyes wide with surprise when he saw, in the middle of all the other rabbits, Great Aunt herself! Her hair was ruffled and she was limping slightly, but otherwise she seemed none the worse for her adventure.

" But the Fox . . . ? " Sultan gasped.

The old rabbit was coming towards him, and now she smiled and bowed her head in a kindly, condescending way.

"Well done, Sultan!" she said. "We must congratulate you on your presence of mind." Then turning to the other rabbits she went on: "I was telling you how the Fox appeared on the hedge. It was then that Sultan showed himself master of the situation in a most admirable way. If he had hesitated a moment all would have been lost. But he did not. With great presence of mind he leapt and ran, leading the Fox away from where I lay. The creature followed him, and so I was safe—safe until this most courageous rabbit could send you all to my help."

"Well done, Sultan!" called one of the rabbits in the crowd. "Three cheers for Sultan!" and, for the next few minutes, to the amazement of the dazed white rabbit in their midst, the rabbits cheered and cheered again until the Warren echoed with their shouts.

CHAPTER XI

ON THE ROAD

" COME for a ramble," suggested Bobbin.

Sultan agreed eagerly.

" I'd love to ! " he said. They had been in all the evening, busy doing odd jobs in Bobbin's house, and now the sun had set and the stars were shining brightly out of a cloudless sky.

Sultan enjoyed these rambles. He felt safe going with Bobbin, and from him learnt much that a wild rabbit has to know—things about Stoats, Weasels, and Foxes, snares and where they were to be found, and, above all, the law by which all the rabbits of the Warren lived—when in danger, *run*.

There were plenty of rabbits about when they came out of the doorway. Nodding to Scuttle, waving friendly paws towards Skurry, they made their way up through the wood, over the top of the hill, and into the fields beyond.

" Shall I show you the way to the Sand Burrow that I visited the other day ? " suggested Bobbin. " Would that be a good idea ? "

Sultan thought that it would. Last time Bobbin asked him he had refused, but this was a very different matter. Bobbin knew the way now—Sultan would like to go with him.

It was a long distance to the Sand Burrow. Over the fields they went, climbing up hedges, scrambling down the other side, running along ditches, and once following a rippling stream for the length of several fields.

" We have to cross a road here," said Bobbin at last. " Things come along the road, large things that hoot and roar, with great bright eyes that glare at you out of the night."

Sultan didn't like the sound of this at all. It seemed a mistake to have to cross that road. From the high bank on which they stood they looked down upon it, clear and deserted, stretching far away on either side of them.

" It's all right ! " said Bobbin. " There's nothing coming. We can cross now quite safely. Oh, wait a minute ! Here's such a lovely dandelion ! "

But Sultan didn't want to wait. If the road was clear now was the time to cross. There were plenty of dandelions everywhere. Probably they were just as good on the far side of the road.

" I'm going on ! " he cried, running down the bank. " I'll wait for you on the other side."

At the bottom of the bank Sultan paused and looked

first to the right and then to the left, up and down the
long stretch of road that lay before him. No ! Bobbin
had been right !   There was nothing coming—no roaring
monster with glittering eyes—all was silent, calm and
peaceful as the night itself. Bravely Sultan stepped
down on to the road.

"Very muddy ! " muttered Sultan to himself.   It
was most odd.   There had been no rain for the last few
days.   The fields and hedges were dry and hard, but
here on the road the ground was soft and sticky and most
unpleasant to walk upon.   There was a queer smell
about the road, too, which Sultan had never met before
and didn't like at all.   Sultan wriggled his nose dis-
gustedly.   Bobbin had never told him of this ! Surely
there was some other way they could have gone !

The white rabbit was almost in the centre of the road
by this time.   With every step he took the ground grew
softer and stickier, and the smell which he so much disliked was now so strong as to be almost overpowering.
Sultan thought that roads were very nasty things to walk
upon.   It was such horrid stuff to wade through—
blacker and more clinging than any mud he had ever
seen.   He could hardly get his feet out—it was getting
deeper—he *couldn't* get his feet out !

Sultan stopped a moment to rest, and it was that
pause that was his undoing.   He was a heavy rabbit, and
his weight drove him a little deeper into the sticky black
slime—just the little bit that made the difference.   When

Sultan tried to move on again he found that each one of his four feet had stuck firmly to the ground.

"Help! Bobbin! No! Don't come on here! I can't move!"

At the frightened cry from his friend, Bobbin left the dandelion he was eating and hurried down to the edge of the road.

"What is it? What's the matter? What's this funny smell?"

Bobbin peered anxiously out from among the long grass at the edge of the road. What could have happened? Whatever was Sultan doing, standing there squeaking with fear in the middle of the road? Why didn't he come back? Why didn't he move?

"Don't touch the road!" shouted Sultan over his shoulder. "It's horrid! My feet have stuck and I can't move! It feels horrid, and it smells horrid, and I wish I'd never come!"

Bobbin couldn't understand it at all. The road looked quite different from when he had last seen it, and this smell, this queer smell, what could it all mean? Suddenly Bobbin remembered a warning he had once had—suddenly he realized what had happened.

"I know!" he called out excitedly. "I know what it is! It's tar! I've never seen it before, but Great Aunt told us that they sometimes put it on roads. It's very dangerous to rabbits! Can't you possibly get yourself free?"

Sultan tried. He pulled and he struggled and he kicked, but his efforts merely made him sink deeper, become more firmly stuck in the clutch of the newly tarred road. Eyes wide with horror, pushing his way through the grass in order to see Sultan's every movement, Bobbin watched the struggle.

"Perhaps I could pull you off," he suggested doubtfully. "I might make a carpet of leaves, dock leaves or something large, and then I'd be able to get to you."

"I'm sure you couldn't!" sobbed the white rabbit. "I'm much too heavy."

This was quite true. Sultan *was* heavy, and Bobbin

little more than half his size. He could never pull him
off alone.

" I shall have to go for help ! " he shouted back.

Bobbin felt worried. He didn't like it at all. They
were a long way from the Warren and it was some time
since they had met a single rabbit. It wasn't safe to
leave Sultan alone in the middle of the dangerous road,
and yet if Bobbin stayed how was he to get help ? No !
There was nothing else to be done. He couldn't pull
Sultan off by himself, and there'd be no rabbits to help him
unless he went to fetch them. The sooner he started
the better.

" I'm going now ! Don't struggle any more or you'll
sink further in. I'll be back as soon as I can, and then
we'll soon get you off ! " and, turning away, Bobbin
raced up the bank as fast as he could go.

Sultan said nothing. He wished Bobbin wouldn't
go. He didn't like being left alone. He remembered
those monsters Bobbin had spoken of—huge things that
rushed roaring along the road, hooting as they went,
with great glaring eyes. Again he struggled furiously,
but with no result. Sultan grew more and more frightened and miserable. Why had he ever come ? Why had
he ever left the Warren ? Why had he ever left the Shed ?
Why didn't Bobbin *hurry* ?

Bobbin was hurrying. He was running as fast as a
rabbit could go—over fields, over hedges, jumping ditches,
ears back, legs scampering over the ground—back to the

Warren and help.   He had hoped to meet some of the
rabbits on the way.   Other nights they passed plenty,
rabbits seemed to pop up from under every hedge, but
to-night there was not a rabbit to be seen.

He was within sight of the Warren doorway when at
last, jumping down from a hedge, he landed almost on
top of Skurry and Scuttle, who were cropping the grass
in the field below.   Panting and breathless, thinking of
the frightened rabbit he had left behind him, Bobbin
gasped out his story.

" There's no time to lose," he ended.   " We must
go at once.   Anything might happen to him at any
moment."

Skurry and Scuttle quite agreed.

" You rest for a minute or two," said Skurry, " and
we'll find help."

Then, leaving their meal, they scampered off and in
a very few moments had collected quite an army of
rabbits ready to follow Bobbin back to the road and to
the rescue of Sultan.   Only too anxious to be off Bobbin
led the way, silently hurrying on in front of the others
until at last the shining, treacherous road was in sight.

" It's down here !   This is the way we went—down
by the ivy-covered oak tree."

Down the bank the rabbits scrambled, one after the
other, looking eagerly over the top of the grass at the
road before them.

" Where is he ? "

" Where's Sultan ? "

" Which way did he go ? "

For a moment Bobbin stopped, a puzzled frown on his face.

" This *is* the right place ! " he said. " I know it is. Yes ! Here's the very dandelion I was eating ! "

He had led the rabbits to the right spot. There was no doubt at all about that. Before them a few grains of earth kicked down on to the tar showed where Sultan had first stepped on to the road. Yes! The place was right but, look as they might, there was no white rabbit on the road ! Sultan had gone—vanished completely while Bobbin was away, leaving not so much as a tuft of white fur behind. In the middle of the road a disturbed smear of tar showed that something had happened there—*something*, but *what* ?

Sadly the group of rabbits stood looking at the empty road. They all realized from what Bobbin had said that Sultan could never have freed himself—and yet he was no longer there. Something terrible must have happened to him. Not a rabbit mentioned Fox. Not one of them said the word " Hawk." Quietly they turned away. In silence they made their way back over the fields. Sultan had gone. That he was lost to them for ever not one of them doubted. They had grown used to Sultan. They had grown fond of Sultan. Sadly and silently the rescue party returned to the Warren.

CHAPTER XII

ESCAPE

" Go on ! " squeaked Angelina excitedly. " Do go on ! You'd got to the part where you had stuck in the tar and that other rabbit had gone to fetch help."

From behind the wire netting of his hutch Sultan, the prize Angora, looked round importantly. This was the kind of thing he liked—respect, admiration, envy. From all the way round the Shed pink eyes, filled with awe and amazement, gazed admiringly at him. With noses pressed to the wire netting, and ears pricked lest they should miss a word of what he was saying, all the rabbits were listening eagerly. Not a sound could be heard. Not a straw rustled in the Shed.

Sultan was enjoying himself immensely. As soon as he thought his dramatic pause had lasted long enough he went on with his story.

" As I was saying," he continued, a little pompously, " there I was, in a most unfortunate position. Bobbin had not been gone long before I heard, away in the distance, a faint roaring sound which gradually grew louder and louder. Straining my eyes in the darkness I looked along the road, and there I saw the most terrifying sight—at least I expect any of you would have called it terrifying."

Angelina gave a little squeak of excitement, but smothered it quickly in case it should interrupt Sultan in his story.

" It certainly was rather alarming," he went on. " A great monster was coming along the road, hooting just as Bobbin had warned me, and looking down upon me with two enormous, yellow, glaring eyes. Nearer and nearer it came until I thought that at any moment I should be crushed beneath its weight, but when it was nearly on top of me it stopped, stood still, and stared and stared at me till I felt quite dazzled, and hardly knew what was happening."

He paused again. Yes, the other rabbits were suitably impressed. Undoubtedly he was the hero of the moment.

" The next thing I can remember," he went on, " was two voices speaking quite close to me. ' Why, it's a white rabbit stuck in the tar,' said one. ' It must have been dazzled by our headlights.' ' It looks to me like one of Jane's Angoras,' said the other. ' Let's take it back and see if she's lost one.' They picked me up— pulled me away with a terrible wrench from the horrible, black, smelling tar—and lifted me inside the great monster I had seen coming down the road. Then we moved on again. I did not care for the journey much. It was something like the trains one travels to the Shows in, but of course I was not in any basket, which was pleasanter. Jane, of course, was delighted to see me when we arrived and, well, here I am!"

A deep sigh of wonder and astonishment rippled round the Shed as Sultan came to the end of his story. Never before had the Angoras heard anything like it. They knew there were other rabbits—they had seen a good many at the various Shows they had been to—they had even heard that there were rabbits who lived a free, wild life in the big Out of Doors, but never had they thought of visiting them, nor dreamed of such wonders as Sultan had to relate.

"Those other rabbits must have thought you a very wonderful creature," said Angelina in a voice filled with admiration. "Did they make you king? Did you rule the Warren?"

For a moment Sultan could think of nothing to say. Just like Angelina to ask a tactless thing like that! Silly rabbit, Angelina! Still it was very nice to be appreciated, to be taken at his true value again. King of the Warren! Sultan thought of Great Aunt and shivered.

"There was no king to the Warren," he said, and went on hurriedly to tell them how he had saved the Warren from fire.

He was only half way through the story when the door opened and in came Jane and Henry.

" Look at Sultan ! " said Jane. " Did you ever see
a rabbit in such a mess ? He's plastered with tar, and
the brown mud from the fields seems to have worked
itself right into his fur ! "

Then followed for Sultan a most unpleasant morning.
It was worse than anything that had happened to him
in the Shed before—nastier than being prepared for a
Show dozens of times over. First they covered him with
butter to get off the tar, then they washed him in hot
water to remove the butter. After that they settled down
with brushes and combs and groomed and groomed him
for what seemed to the uncomfortable rabbit to be hours
on end.

But Sultan did not mind—not *really* mind. He never
grumbled once. A month ago he used to make the most
terrible fuss over the simple preparations for a Show, but
now it was different. Now he knew that all would soon
be well. He was in the Shed—he was safe. However
uncomfortable, however unpleasant things might be at
the moment, they would be bound to end soon and then
all would be well. In the end they would give him a
good meal and leave him alone. Sultan thought of the
terrible moments of imprisonment in the Fox's larder.
He thought of the time when he had struggled frantically
in the snare—of the terrifying experience of being left
alone on the tarred road. No ! Nothing mattered here.
Jane and Henry could do their worst. He was in the
Shed ! He was safe ! Soon all would be well.

Then they washed him.

" Do you think he'll be fit for the Show on Tuesday ? "
asked Jane anxiously.

Henry thought he might.   It would be worth trying,
anyway.

So they were going to show him again, were they ?
Sultan, the prize Angora, could not help feeling relieved.
Deep down in his mind doubts had lately arisen as to
whether he really was the fine fellow, the handsome
rabbit, he had always considered himself to be.   Though
he would never have admitted it, the scorn and lately
the kindly condescension with which he had been treated
at the Warren had left its mark.   Was he, after all, the
finest rabbit in the country ?   Was he the finest in the
Shed ?   Was he even a fine rabbit at all ?

As the day of the Show drew nearer Sultan grew more
and more anxious.   Suppose he should not receive a
prize !   Suppose he should not even be classed !   Sultan
grew silent, jumpy, a very nervous rabbit.

When at last Tuesday arrived and Sultan found himself at the Show, unlike his usual demeanour of careless
arrogance, he followed the judges round with eager,
anxious eyes.   Never had he been so relieved, never so
thankful as when the card announcing First Prize was
pinned upon the front of his hutch.   The rest of the
day passed like a dream, and when he found himself
back in the Shed once more his one longing was that
Bobbin and his other friends at the Warren should know
about it.

"If only I could tell them!" he muttered to himself over and over again. "If only I could show them the certificate, then perhaps they'd understand. Then they might believe that I wasn't the wrong kind of rabbit after all."

The longer he thought about it the greater the hold the idea took upon him. For several days he could think of nothing else, then at last his opportunity came.

"It's so hot, don't you think we might leave the Shed open this afternoon?" suggested Jane, when she and Henry had finished turning out the hutches several days after the Show.

"Yes, I should think so," agreed Henry. "I'm taking Bounce out for a walk now, but I shall be back in a couple of hours. I can shut up then."

A couple of hours! The Shed was to be left open for a couple of hours—and Bounce would be out of the way! Sultan listened to the scrunch of Jane's and Henry's footsteps on the gravel growing fainter and fainter in the distance, then eagerly he pressed his nose down to that weak spot in the wire netting of his hutch. No! All was well! While Sultan was away Henry had not bothered to nail it down but, pushing it roughly into place, had left it as it was. Then, in the excitement of Sultan's return followed immediately by the preparations for the Show, Henry had once more forgotten all about it.

Eagerly Sultan pushed his way out and once again

jumped down on to the floor of the Shed. Standing on tiptoe he was delighted to find that he could just reach the corner of his new First Class Certificate. One tug and it was in his mouth and, taking no notice at all of the excited cries of Angelina and the other rabbits in the Shed, Sultan raced away down the garden path.

A couple of hours Henry had said. He had only a couple of hours to get to the Warren, find the rabbits he wanted to see, and hurry back to the Shed. It was not very long but it might—it must—be time enough.

It was a lucky day for Sultan. When he reached the railway bank he saw to his delight that not only Bobbin and Great Aunt, but nearly all the rabbits of the Warren, were sunning themselves upon the grassy slope.

Though he did not know it, it was of Sultan the rabbits were talking at the moment of his approach.

" It was certainly a very sad affair," Great Aunt was saying. " Poor Sultan ! He was not a clever rabbit, and his looks were certainly peculiar, but we miss him. It is very sad to think of any rabbit disappearing in such a mysterious and suspicious manner."

" *Anything* may have happened to him," said Skurry, in a hushed voice.

" Bobbin has not been the same rabbit since," added Scuttle. " Why, look ! What's he doing now ? "

With a cry of " Sultan ! Sultan ! " Bobbin shot past them. Immediately every rabbit upon the bank stopped eating, every ear was pricked, all eyes gazed expectantly towards the top of the slope, where, to the surprise of all, the white Angora of whom they were speaking had suddenly appeared, waving in his mouth a large red card.

The next moment they were all rushing upwards. Cries of " Sultan! Sultan!" echoed all over the bank—rabbits pushed and crowded against each other, anxious to get to the front, eager to hear the story the white rabbit had to tell.

" We are very pleased to see you alive and well," said Great Aunt. " We should like to hear how you escaped from the tarred road, and where you have been since we last saw you in the Warren."

Sultan told them. He told them of his rescue from the tar. He told them of his return to the Shed. He told them of the Show, and then, keeping his proudest moment till the end, he showed them the certificate which he had carried all the way for them to see.

The rabbits looked at it, puzzled and, thought Sultan, not as much impressed as he had hoped to find them.

" Is it good to eat ? " asked Great Aunt.

" What does it do ? " said Bobbin.

" It's my certificate ! " Sultan wished he could make them understand. " It says I was the best rabbit there."

" But if you *were* the best rabbit there," Great Aunt sounded very doubtful, " why should you need a thing like that to say so ? I don't ! " said Great Aunt simply.

" Never mind ! " said Bobbin kindly, seeing that his

friend seemed disappointed. " We'll take it back to my house. It will be useful as a front door mat."

A front door mat! His certificate—*a front door mat!*

" And after this," Great Aunt was speaking now, " we think it would be best for you not to stray more than

three yards from the mouth of the Warren. Later on, perhaps, when you have learnt a little more wisdom, we may allow you to wander further, but at present . . ."

Great Aunt stopped. She had thought she was addressing a white rabbit, but there was no white rabbit to be seen, no sign at all of Sultan upon the bank.

This was not surprising, for Sultan, the prize Angora,

was now running as hard as he could go through the cornfield, with his precious certificate grasped firmly in his mouth. A couple of hours! Had he stayed too long? Faster and faster he rushed over the ground.

At last he came in sight of the Shed, and was startled by a curious banging noise which seemed to be coming from inside. But it did not stop him—nothing would stop him now. Home and safety were in sight. Home and safety he was going to have. Up the steps he sprang, and the next moment was in the Shed itself.

"There you are!"

Dropping the hammer with which she was nailing down the wire netting at the front of his hutch, Jane sprang forward and pounced on him. For a moment Sultan felt annoyed. It was silly of her to grab like that —couldn't she *see* he was coming back?

Jane picked him up firmly and put him into his hutch—his mended hutch from which there could be no further escape.

"What a fright you gave me!" she went on sternly, "with the best Show of all coming on next week, and you the only rabbit worth entering!"

But Sultan didn't mind. The mended hutch troubled him not at all. Jane might be as cross as she liked. "The best Show of all," she had said. The best Show— and he, and he alone of all the rabbits in the Shed, was being sent to it. This was being treated properly—this was being appreciated. Nobody here despised him!

None of them wanted to make door mats of his precious certificates. Sultan, the prize Angora, shook himself until his glorious white coat stood out magnificently round him, then, closing his eyes, he went happily to sleep.

PRINTED IN GREAT BRITAIN AT
THE PRESS OF THE PUBLISHERS